Once Upon a Prince

Holly Jacobs

Perry
Square

$4.25 U.S.
$4.99 CAN.

Silhouette®

Where love comes alive™

ISBN 0-373-19777-2

9 780373 197774

50425

EAN

Shey Carlson was waiting for a prince.

Not in a she-was-waiting-for-her-personal-prince-charming-to-come-to-her-rescue sort of way. Rather, she was standing in Erie, Pennsylvania's small airport waiting for Prince Eduardo Michael Tanner Ericson of Amar.

A man dressed in an impeccable suit walked through the terminal.

"Your Highness?" Shey asked.

"Marie Anna, you've..." the prince started then paused, obviously searching for something to say. "You've changed since we last met."

Shey looked down at her motorcycle jacket. "I'm not Marie Anna. I'm Shey. Shey Carlson." She thrust out her hand to shake.

The prince ignored it.

Did you curtsy for a prince?

This kind of protocol was never necessary in her neighborhood, and Shey Carlson didn't curtsy or bow to anyone. Not even a real, honest-to-goodness, runs-a-country sort of prince.

* * *

Once Upon a Princess (SR May 2005)
Once Upon a Prince (SR July 2005)
Once Upon a King (SR September 2005)

Dear Reader,

It's two days before Christmas, and while the streets of New York City are teeming with all the sights and sounds of the holiday, here at Silhouette Romance we're putting the finishing touches on our July schedule. In case you're not familiar with publishing, we need that much lead time to produce the romances you enjoy.

And, of course, I can't help boasting already about the great lineup we've planned for you. Popular author Susan Meier heads the month with *Baby Before Business* (SR #1774), in which an all-work Scrooge gets his priorities in order when he discovers love with his PR executive-turned-nanny. The romance kicks off the author's new baby-themed trilogy, BRYANT BABY BONANZA. Carol Grace continues FAIRY-TALE BRIDES with *Cinderellie!* (SR #1775), in which a millionaire goes in search of the beautiful caterer who's left her slipper behind in his mansion. *A Bride for a Blue-Ribbon Cowboy* (SR #1776) introduces Silhouette Special Edition author Judy Duarte to the line. Part of the new BLOSSOM COUNTY FAIR miniseries, this romance involves a tomboy's transformation to win the cowboy of her dreams. Finally, Holly Jacobs continues her PERRY SQUARE miniseries with *Once Upon a Prince* (SR #1777), featuring the town's beloved redheaded rebel and a royal determined to woo and win her!

And don't miss next month's selection led by reader favorites Judy Christenberry and Patricia Thayer.

Happy reading!

Ann Leslie Tuttle
Associate Senior Editor

Please address questions and book requests to:
Silhouette Reader Service
U.S.: 3010 Walden Ave., P.O. Box 1325, Buffalo, NY 14269
Canadian: P.O. Box 609, Fort Erie, Ont. L2A 5X3

Once Upon a Prince

Holly Jacobs

Perry Square

SILHOUETTE *Romance*®

Published by Silhouette Books

America's Publisher of Contemporary Romance

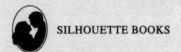 SILHOUETTE BOOKS

ISBN 0-373-19777-2

ONCE UPON A PRINCE

Printed in U.S.A.

Books by Holly Jacobs

Silhouette Romance

Do You Hear What I Hear? #1557
A Day Late and a Bride Short #1653
Dad Today, Groom Tomorrow #1683
Be My Baby #1733
†*Once Upon a Princess* #1768
†*Once Upon a Prince* #1777

†Perry Square: The Royal Invasion!

HOLLY JACOBS

can't remember a time when she didn't read…and read a lot. Writing her own stories just seemed a natural outgrowth of that love. Reading, writing, chauffeuring kids to and from activities makes for a busy life. But it's one she wouldn't trade for any other.

Holly lives in Erie, Pennsylvania, with her husband, four children and a 180-pound Old English Mastiff. In her "spare" time, Holly loves hearing from her fans. You can write to her at P.O. Box 11102, Erie, PA 16514-1102 or visit her Web site at www.HollysBooks.com.

Dear Reader,

Shey Carlson is my rebel with a cause. She believes one person can make a difference. Her passion for life and her constant support of friends made her a wonderful character to create. She also supports causes and one of them is literacy—not just the ability to read functionally, but the ability to find magic in stories. Reading has been my lifelong pleasure. In fact, it's given me the world. And learning to read for the love of story, that's a true gift that Shey tries to share.

And who else would there be for her to share it with, than Tanner Ericson, a true prince of a guy!

I hope you enjoy this second book in the Perry Square royalty trilogy. I'd love to hear from you at www.Hollysbooks.com or P.O. Box 11102, Erie, PA, 16514-1102.

Holly

Chapter One

Shey Carlson was waiting for a prince.

Not in a waiting-for-her-personal-Prince-Charming-to-come-riding-to-her-rescue sort of way; rather she was standing in the small airport in Erie, Pennsylvania, waiting for a real, honest-to-goodness royal runs-a-country sort of prince.

Prince Eduardo Matthew Tanner Ericson of Amar to be exact. The unwanted fiancé of Parker Dillon—Shey's best friend—to be even more exact.

How a girl from humble beginnings ended up waiting to greet a prince was a bit of a mystery. But then it was no more mysterious than the fact that the same girl had a princess as one of her best friends.

A man dressed in an impeccable suit, with perfectly styled dark brown hair and an ultrawhite smile, walked through the terminal door surrounded by three large men with serious expressions. Bodyguards, their stances practically screamed. The trio scanned the area, alert for any hidden danger.

The tallest guard had a thin, muscular build and dark skin, the middle-size one, who was still akin to a giant, was bulkier, and had more of a wrestler's build and a crew-cut. The third was Asian, with a wiry, lean body. He winked at her as they approached and shot her a thousand-watt smile that Shey was sure worked on most women.

She scowled her response.

Shey Carlson was not most women.

The prince had arrived with his entourage.

"Your Highness?" Shey asked, though she didn't need to. This man's mere presence shouted royalty, just as the other three radiated come on and try something.

"Marie Anna, you've…" the prince started then paused, obviously searching for something to say. "You've changed since we last met."

Shey looked down at her leather jacket.

She couldn't imagine Parker wearing anything like it. Not that Parker was prone to wearing a tiara and ball gown, but she wasn't the leather-jacket type, either.

"Since I'm not Marie Anna—who, by the way, goes by the name Parker these days—I guess *change* is an accurate word." She thrust out her hand to shake. "Shey. Shey Carlson."

The prince ignored her gesture. He was probably more accustomed to people bowing to him and kissing his ring.

Wait a minute, wasn't it the higher-up clergy who expected ring-kissing?

Did you curtsy to a prince?

This kind of protocol had never been necessary in her lower East Side neighborhood when she was growing up. But whatever it was she was supposed to do, the handshake was the best she had to offer.

Shey Carlson didn't curtsy or bow to anyone, and she certainly wasn't into ring-kissing.

Not even for a handsome prince.

"You're not Marie Anna...Parker?" He scanned the crowd. "Do you mind if I inquire where my fiancée is?"

"Ah, there is another little problem," Shey said. "You see, Parker's not your fiancée."

Mr. Ultrawhite-smile wasn't smiling now. He frowned. "That's not what our betrothal papers say. Not what her father says, either."

"Unless you're planning to marry her father, I figure it doesn't matter what he says, or what some papers say. Parker's not your fiancée."

"Why don't you allow *Parker*," he drew the name out with obvious distaste, "and I to settle this. Where is she?"

"She doesn't want to see you, that's why she asked me to pick you up."

"And I insist you take me to her." There was a small tic on the left side of his upper lip.

Did it indicate annoyance?

Shey sure hoped so.

"Fine," she said with a shrug. "But I don't have room for your gargoyles on my bike."

"Bike?" he asked, ignoring the gargoyle comment altogether.

"My Harley. You're welcome to a ride if you like. The three stooges here can grab your luggage and meet you at the hotel later."

"Your Highness—" the largest stooge started to protest.

"It's fine, Emil," Tanner said with a regal nod of dismissal.

Emil obviously wasn't intimidated. He didn't back down. "Your father would be very displeased if we let you go off with a stranger."

The prince gave Shey a quick once-over and turned back to Quasimodo. "I think I can handle her."

"I don't know, Your Highness, maybe you'd better let me handle her for you," the ladykiller body-guard said in a low, sultry tone.

"You know Peter has a way with women," the mid-dle-size brute added.

"That's enough, Tonio. I'll handle our unexpected hostess myself."

Shey couldn't help it…she laughed. "Better men than you have tried to handle me."

"Did they succeed?" Tanner asked, a hint of a smile playing on his lips.

Shey shook her head. "Not a one."

"Why doesn't that surprise me?" This time the smile wasn't a hint, it was full-blown and quite a sight to behold.

If Shey was prone to let looks influence her, her knees would be decidedly weak at the sight of that smile. But she wasn't prone in that sense, so she stood quite solidly on the ground despite the fact this prince was easily the sexiest man she'd seen in a very long time.

A very, very long time.

He turned back to his henchmen. "I'll meet you at the hotel in a short while."

"Your Highness," Tonio objected, obviously ready to start another argument.

"Tonio, not another word."

And without another word to Curly, Mo and Larry,

the prince turned to Shey and said, "I'm ready to see my fiancée."

"You're in for a treat."

She led him out of the small airport without another word. She smiled as they reached her baby.

"This is it," she announced, running a hand over the red tank.

She knew there was pride in her voice. She couldn't help it. Her father had died when she was five and she didn't have many memories of him. But she did have a distinct one—it was like a snapshot in her head—of her father, sitting on a flaming red Harley and smiling. A young man with a family who loved him, his whole life in front of him.

"This is our vehicle?" the prince asked, sounding less than enthused.

"No. A Harley is not a vehicle. It's a bike, a hog, a way of life, but not a vehicle. That's too plain, too mundane a word to describe a Harley."

"You love this bike." It was a statement, not a question.

"Yeah, I do."

She wasn't embarrassed by the fact. She'd worked hard to buy the bike. It was more than a memory, more than transportation. The Harley represented how far she'd come from the little girl wearing hand-me-down clothes at school.

"But it's simply a way of getting from one place to another." He looked confused.

"A Harley is more than simply a method of going from one place to another."

He shook his head.

"Have you ever ridden one of these?" Shey asked, though she was pretty sure she knew the answer.

"No."

"Then let me teach you a thing or two."

Shey got her spare helmet off the back and handed it to His Royal Cluelessness. "Here, put this on."

She expected him to fuss that it would mess his perfect hair, that it wasn't cool to wear a helmet, but the prince simply put it on.

Even though Pennsylvania had recently rescinded its helmet requirements, Shey was still a stickler for them. She slipped on her own helmet, slid her leg over the seat and started the bike.

It roared to life.

"Okay, climb on behind me," she practically shouted in order to be heard over the rumble of the engine.

The prince did as instructed. His body pressed tightly against hers. His arms wrapped around her waist.

A small shiver of something crept up Shey's spine.

It had been months since any man had touched her. Her reaction to the prince was simply a hormonal thing. Nothing more.

She kicked the bike into gear and started toward 12th Street.

"Hang on," she called and she slipped into second, then quickly into third gear.

The feel of wind rushing against her face, the speed…riding the bike never failed to soothe her. But there was something different tonight—the man whose arms were wrapped lightly around her waist. The effect wasn't quite as soothing as normal. As a matter of fact, there was a strange sensation that twisted her stomach and left her feeling short of breath.

Shey ignored it and simply concentrated on taking the prince to Monarch's.

She'd let Parker deal with him.

Parker would send the prince packing and things would get back to normal.

Parker, Cara and Shey, three college friends, worked together at the coffeehouse, Monarch's, and Titles Bookstore. No guys to muddle things up.

Shey remembered the night they'd come up with the names for their two attached stores. Parker had supplied the financial backing for the venture and they'd wanted to do something to acknowledge their royal friend. They'd all three laughed as they passed the bottle of wine and talked about the future—theirs and the stores'.

Shey had never had women friends before Parker and Cara, but if she'd been asked who'd she'd pick as friends, she would never have said a princess and someone like Cara, a quiet, soft-hearted woman.

Truth be told, when it came down to it, she hadn't picked Parker and Cara at all...they'd simply meshed. Three people who'd connected and become friends. Friends who were closer than most families.

The prince's arms tightened ever so slightly, reminding Shey of her unwanted passenger, jolting her from her thoughts.

Tanner Ericson knew that coming to Erie and collecting his fiancée was going to be a challenge. Marie Anna's father had told him she might be a bit reluctant.

He'd prepared himself for all kinds of scenarios. But never in his wildest imagination had he thought he'd be whizzing down the city streets on the back of a motorbike driven by a most intriguing woman.

Short, spiky red hair and an attitude that screamed back off. This Shey Carlson was a tough, beautiful woman.

He inched a bit closer and tightened his arms around her waist, not so much because he was worried about falling off her motorbike, but because he liked the way she felt against him.

Eventually she turned off the four-lane street

they'd been riding on, and much too soon they were pulling up to the curb.

She cut the motor and Tanner climbed off the bike. He took off his helmet and handed it to her.

"This is it," she said.

He could hear in her voice that this place, with its small brick storefront, was special to her. The building had two doors. Over the right-hand one was a sign that read, Monarch's Coffeehouse. It had a small crown tilted over the *M*.

The other sign read, Titles Bookstore. The same crown was over it, as well.

"Marie Anna's here?"

"*Parker* owns the stores, along with *Cara* and myself. We're all partners." Shey started toward Monarch's. "Come, on, Your Highness."

He was accustomed to being called Your Highness but he preferred going by Tanner. Of course, he understood the necessity of his title or a more formal means of address when in Amar. But he was in America now. There was no need to stand on formalities here. Not with this woman.

"Tanner," he said. "Call me Tanner."

She didn't say anything, just kept right on walking.

There was nothing for Tanner to do but follow.

He entered Monarch's and found a blond woman talking to a dark-haired man.

It had to be her—Marie Anna.

He studied the woman he'd pledged to marry.

She hadn't changed all that much. Yes, she looked less styled: her blond hair was pulled into a messy ponytail and she had on a pair of neat khaki pants and a light blue top.

This was the woman he was going to spend the rest of his life with.

Tanner still had a hard time swallowing the fact that he had agreed to marry a woman he really didn't know. But it was for the good of Amar.

He'd been lectured since birth that his first obligation was to his country. Small principalities like Amar and Marie Anna's Eliason, could easily become lost in today's world. By joining forces, the two small countries might have more clout. So in the age-old custom, he'd allowed himself to become engaged for political purposes.

At least, in public that was the reason he gave. In truth, he was just tired. Tired of women who merely wanted his title, his money. Women who thought they wanted to play princess, until they realized being a princess entailed very little play and an awful lot of hard work.

He was done.

After Stephana, he'd realized he'd never have a normal relationship with a woman, one built on mutual respect and—well, he wouldn't admit it out loud, but the romantic in him craved a relationship based on love. But he'd simply come to the conclusion that it wouldn't happen. That's why he'd agreed to marry Marie Anna—Parker. She understood the intricacies of being a royal in modern society. Their union would be good for their countries.

If he couldn't have what he wanted, then he'd settle for doing something that would be beneficial for Amar.

"Princess Marie Anna," he said.

She stared at him and frowned.

"It's Parker," was her reply. "It's been a long time, Tanner."

"Too long," he said, smiling at her.

There was no answering smile, as a matter of fact, her frown deepened to a scowl.

Two beautiful women had scowled at him in the last hour. Tanner didn't like it.

"Not long enough," she muttered.

Okay, so the pleasantries had been dealt with, time to lay his cards on the table. "Your father sent me to bring you home."

"I am home."

Tanner didn't remember Marie Anna—Parker—as being so stubborn.

"Back to Eliason," he clarified.

"You're welcome to go back to Eliason or Amar on the very next plane out of Erie. But I'm staying here."

"That's it?" he asked. "I flew all this way to see my fiancée—"

"I am not your fiancée."

He could hear the finality in her voice, but ignored her comment altogether and continued. "—and all you have to say to me is leave?"

"That's about the shape of things. And speaking of leaving, I'm on my way out. You don't mind closing up, Shey?"

"Of course not," Shey said.

Tanner had almost forgotten about his bike-riding escort.

Almost, but not quite.

He was pretty sure that having met Shey Carlson, no one could ever entirely forget her.

Shey nodded in his direction and asked Marie Anna, "What about him?"

"Would you give him a ride to whatever hotel he's staying at?" she asked.

"Sure," Shey said with a shrug.

"Hey, watchdog, are you coming?" Parker asked the dark-haired man who'd been silent till now.

"Uh," was his terribly articulate response. "Sure thing," he said. "How about I drive?"

"Sounds good to me since I took the bus."

"The bus?" Tanner asked. "My fiancée is riding public transportation?"

First Parker sends Shey to collect him at the airport, then she denies their engagement and now she was talking about riding a bus to work?

"You don't have a fiancée," Parker replied, "but if you were referring to me, then yes, I take public transportation. My father shut off my access to my trust and I'm broke. So I sold the car."

"But, but…" he said, not sure what to add.

"Don't worry about it," the other man said. "I'll see that she gets home all right."

"Home," Parker said to Tanner. "I'm home and you need to go home. Go back to Amar. There's nothing for you here in Erie—especially not a fiancée."

She walked out of the store followed by the dark-haired man.

The door slammed behind them with a certain sense of finality.

"Well, princy, that went well."

"Tanner. My name is Tanner. If you can't remember that, and insist on addressing me formally, Your Highness will suffice. Princy does not."

Shey laughed. "Don't get your boxers in a knot, princy."

"Is it over?" came a soft voice from a small archway that led into what had to be the bookstore.

The woman was shorter than Shey. Curvier. Her hair was brown and she wore it in a simple shoulder-length bob.

"It's over," Shey said. "Cara, this is Parker's supposed Prince Charming. I use the word *supposed* because so far, I haven't found him all that charming."

"Tanner," he said. "Please, call me Tanner, Miss…"

"Phillips. Cara Phillips, but Cara's fine."

"Cara," he said, rolling the *R* slightly. "It's a lovely name."

"Thank you," she said, smiling at him. "I'm sorry you had to come all this way for nothing, Tanner."

"It's not for nothing. Parker will be going home with me."

"She agreed?" Cara asked, looking surprised.

"No," Shey snapped.

"But she will eventually," Tanner added. "She'll see that our marrying makes sense."

"Do you love her?" Cara asked.

"Pardon?" Tanner replied.

"It's a simple question, Your High—Tanner. Do you love Parker?"

"Marie Anna, uh, Parker, and I are extremely well-suited. We both grew up knowing we have a duty to our countries. We were friendly when we were younger. I'm sure we'd be compatible."

"Compatible is nice," Cara said, taking a step closer, her expression earnest as she continued, "but love is important. Do you love her?"

"I'll learn to love her." Even as Tanner said the words, he hoped they were true. He wouldn't want his child, their future children, growing up in a loveless home.

"I know that there are any number of things you can learn," Cara said. "Most things, in fact, you can learn with simply a good mind and a good book. But love? You can't learn to love someone, you can't just study them hard enough and discover you love them. There has to be a spark, something to build on. You'd know if you and Parker had it. We'd know if you had it. You don't."

Tanner had thought he liked Parker's friend Cara far more than Shey, but as she voiced his hidden fear, he found he much preferred Shey's cut-to-the-chase comments to Cara's softer, more insightful ones.

"How dare you walk in and think you can know what I feel?" he asked, assuming his best royal tone, one that was guaranteed to make people think twice before arguing with him.

But Cara didn't back down. Didn't even blink. "I dare because Parker is my friend. I dare because I've seen what a compatible relationship looks like. I dare because I may not know you, but I do know that having power and money doesn't make a person happy, love does. You deserve that as much as Parker does."

"I—"

She cut him off with a small, soft smile. "Good night, Shey. I was ready to lock up next door when the commotion started. Now that it's over, I'll be going. I'll see you in the morning. And it was nice meeting you, Tanner."

With that, Cara turned and walked back into the dim bookstore.

"Wow," Shey said. "I wonder what's got into her?"

"What do you mean?" Tanner asked.

"I mean, that's the longest string of words that I've ever heard Cara utter in front of a stranger. In front of most people she knows well, for that matter."

"Lucky me," Tanner grumbled.

He'd like to totally discount everything the woman had said as nonsense, but he couldn't. She hadn't said anything he hadn't thought himself.

"So now what?" he asked his reluctant hostess.

"Now, I'm going to pour you a cup of coffee and close up the shop. Then I'll take you to your hotel. Tomorrow, if you're smart, you'll be on a plane leaving Erie."

Tanner didn't reply. He didn't know what to say, but he knew that he wasn't ready to leave Erie just yet.

Shey brought him the coffee, then bustled around

the store turning off coffee machines, cleaning out carafes, then gathering up the sandwiches and snacks from the refrigerated case.

She hefted a tray full of items.

"Here, let me help you," he said, as he started to rise from his seat.

"I don't need help," she snapped. "I'm quite capable of handling this on my own."

"Fine," he said, sinking back into the seat as she took the tray and disappeared into the back.

Cara's words played over again in his mind.

She was right, love was an essential ingredient in a marriage, an ingredient his parents' marriage had been lacking.

Tanner realized that Shey had been gone more than a few minutes. He got up and walked toward the kitchen, inching the door open slowly to see what she was doing.

He expected her to be cleaning or something, instead, she was standing at the back door, the tray of food now nearly empty.

There were people lined up and she was handing out the sandwiches and cookies.

"Leo," she said, "did you go to the clinic about that cough?"

An old man wearing tattered clothes, said something softly that Tanner couldn't make out.

"Good," Shey said. "If you hadn't, I'd have dragged you there tomorrow. You'd have had to ride on the back of my bike."

The man laughed at that, the laughter punctuated by a harsh, rasping cough.

"You be sure you go to the shelter tonight. I don't care how warm it is. You need to sleep inside and take your medicine."

The old man nodded, then moved aside, replaced by a younger, yet equally disheveled-looking man.

Slowly, Tanner let the door close and went back to his seat.

He might not have known Shey Carlson long, but he knew she'd resent his witnessing her act of kindness.

Nonetheless it intrigued him.

Shey intrigued him.

No matter what she thought, Tanner wasn't getting on a plane in the morning.

As a matter of fact, he wasn't going back to the hotel tonight.

He pulled out his cell phone and keyed in Emil's number.

"Yeah, boss?"

"You all have the night off," he told his guard.

"What do you mean, night off?" Emil asked, displeasure in his voice.

"I won't be coming to the hotel tonight."

"May I ask where you'll be spending the night?"

"No, you may not."

Emil laughed. "Fine, I won't ask. I'm nothing if not discreet. I'll let Tonio and Peter hit the town. Peter's dying to introduce himself to the female residents."

"I imagine he is," Tanner said with a hint of laughter. Peter was a ladies' man.

"I'll be in all night though, boss," Emil assured him. "If you have any problems, you call. You know your father would have a fit if he found out you were wandering about a strange city without a bodyguard."

Shey walked into the room and Tanner smiled, "I think I can handle myself, Emil."

Emil, more of a friend than a guard, just sighed. "But I'm here if you need me."

"Thanks." Tanner shut the phone and put it in his pocket.

"Are you ready to go?" Shey asked.

"I'm ready," he answered, rising from his seat.

Tanner Ericson was more than ready, but he wasn't sure Shey Carlson was.

Chapter Two

Fifteen minutes later, Shey punched Parker's number into the phone as she glared at the man sitting in her recliner, staring out her living-room window.

Shey knew that Parker had caller ID, so she wasn't surprised when her friend's salutation was, "Thanks for picking up Tanner."

"There's a problem," Shey told Parker without preamble.

The problem heard her and simply smiled.

"What now?" Parker asked. "Who else could my father send?"

If it were only as simple as dealing with Parker's

father. Shey and Cara had years of experience helping their friend circumvent her father's dictates.

"Not your father, your prince," Shey told her.

There was a small sigh of relief before Shey asked,
"Okay, so what did Tanner do?"

"It's what he didn't do…he didn't leave."

"And I'm not going to," Tanner said softly.

Shey put a hand over the receiver and said, "Listening to other people's conversations is just rude. I'd
have expected better from a prince."

"I live to shake people's expectations," he said
with an unprincely grin.

"What do you mean?" Parker asked over the phone.

"I mean, His Royal Painness and his goons—"

"His goons?" Parker asked.

Shey realized she hadn't had a chance to mention
Tanner's three henchmen, so she explained, "He
brought bodyguards, three of them. Anyway, they
have rooms at the new hotel on the bayfront, but
princy here won't go. He says he's staying with me."

"Why on earth would he want to stay with you?"

"Because he said he figured you'd come rescue me
and he'd get to talk to you."

"Do you need me to rescue you?" Parker asked.

Shey had spent her life taking care of herself, not
simply because it was her nature, but because it was
necessity. After her father died, her mother worked at

least two jobs to keep food on the table and a roof over their heads. Shey had to learn to be self-sufficient, because if she hadn't learned to look out for herself, no one else would have.

That all changed when she won an academic scholarship to Mercyhurst College. That's when she'd learned to count on others—when she found Parker and Cara.

No, she took that back. She hadn't found them, they'd found her. She'd never quite figured out how or why, but over the years she discovered it didn't matter. No matter how different they were, they fit. Three pieces that just clicked.

She had people to count on. Her friendship with Parker and Cara had seen to that.

Shey knew if she asked, Parker would come running to help even though the last person she wanted to deal with was her supposed fiancé. Knowing there was someone who would come when you called, no matter what, was a wonderful feeling. And every now and then it hit Shey and she felt a warm glow.

"No," she said with a chuckle. "I just wanted to see how nice I have to be. He's your fiancé, after all."

"No," Parker corrected, "he's an old childhood friend, not a fiancé. And you don't have to be nice at all."

"Really?" Shey asked, smiling at Tanner who had

the good sense to look a bit nervous. He rose and held out his hand for the phone.

"Really," Parker answered.

"Great." Shey ignored Tanner's hand, still raised and waiting for the phone.

"Just don't do anything that will land either of us in jail," Parker added. "I could probably get diplomatic immunity, but you'd be sunk."

"No problem. Hang on, princy wants to talk to you."

"Parker, it's imperative we speak," Tanner insisted.

He was quiet as he listened to whatever Parker responded.

"Parker," he said, "your father said—"

Parker must have cut him off because he stopped in midsentence.

"Someone else? Who?" He didn't wait for her to answer. "That man from tonight?"

Shey almost felt sorry for Tanner. Parker was a dangerous opponent.

She'd remembered what had happened to poor Hoffman—the last man Parker's father had sent after her. Parker had fixed up Hoffman with Perry Square's resident manicurist, Josie. Hoffman swore it was a vicious, horrible act of spite. He'd had to spend so much time evading Josie and her pals, that he hadn't been able to properly tail the runaway princess. Eventually, he'd told Parker's father he quit, but by then he'd become accustomed to Josie, that they became one of the Square's newest, happiest couples.

Maybe she should warn Tanner what he was up against.

Shey glanced at the very disgruntled-looking prince, who refused to leave her home, and quickly decided that maybe she shouldn't.

"You can't be serious," Tanner said.

He waited a moment longer, then hung up the phone.

"So?" Shey asked.

"She's seeing someone else?" he asked.

Shey knew Parker wasn't, but she was willing to play along for her friend's sake. "It never occurred to you that someone as amazing as Parker would be dating?"

"No."

He looked as if the whole concept of a woman preferring someone other than himself was not only distasteful, but was totally incomprehensible.

"Well, princy, you're not as bright as you think you are. Men are always after Parker. Chasing her, wooing her. I think it shows an awful lot of conceit to think she'd be just sitting here waiting for you."

The momentary look of confusion disappeared and a regal arrogance took its place. "Speaking of waiting, I'm waiting for you to show me to the guest room. I had a long flight, a long day. I need to get some rest."

"There is no guest room," Shey said. Even if there had been she wouldn't have told the prince. Let him tough it out. Maybe he'd give up and leave.

"Where do your guests normally sleep?" he asked.

"I don't have guests."

"Family?"

Shey felt a small stab of regret for what she didn't have, then reminded herself that she was lucky in what she did have.

"Parker and Cara are my only family," she said, "and they have their own places, so no sleepovers."

"But surely this little place has more than one bedroom."

She sighed and said, "*Surely* the place does have another bedroom, but I converted it into an office since I don't have guests."

"Does your office have a couch?" he asked hopefully.

"No," Shey said with a smile. "It has a desk, it has bookshelves, it even has some file cabinets, but no couch."

"Then I guess I'll be sleeping down here." He frowned at the leather sofa.

Shey would bet a big wad of cash that princy had never slept on a couch in his entire life.

Heck he'd probably never even slept on a twin bed. It was all king-size mattresses for the prince, she was sure.

"No," she said patiently. "You'll be going back to your hotel and sleeping there in your nice, spacious penthouse suite."

She wasn't sure if the new hotel had a penthouse suite, but if it did, that's where the prince would be staying.

"Come on," she urged. "You've had your fun, but this plan isn't going to work. Parker's going to stay as far away from me as possible, at least until I shake you. So call one of your henchmen to come pick you up, or if you prefer, I can call you a taxi."

"If Parker is your family, as you claim, then she won't be able to stay away for very long. She'll eventually come to your rescue. And when she does, she'll find me waiting to talk to her."

"You're not spending the night," Shey said with mounting frustration. She felt a totally out-of-character urge to stomp her foot. She caught herself prestomp and settled for crossing her arms over her chest.

"I'm going to undress now," the prince said with a smile. "Of course, you're welcome to stay, if you like."

"Threatening to undress in front a stranger." She shook her head and tsked. "And you an engaged man, and all."

He pulled off his jacket and reached for the buttons on his shirt.

"You wouldn't," she said.

"Try me."

She felt a tug of curiosity and realized that if the man unbuttoning his shirt hadn't been a prince—a prince who thought he was engaged to her best friend—she'd be very tempted to *try* him.

Instead of staying for the show, she turned and said, "Fine. I'm leaving."

"Oh, do you have a pillow and blanket I can use?"

Do you have a pillow and blanket, he asked in the condescending princy tone. As if someone who didn't have a mansion or a guest room wouldn't be able to come up with even a pillow and blanket for a guest.

An uninvited guest, but a guest nonetheless.

How on earth had she found herself in this situation?

Truth was, she *didn't* have a spare blanket or pillow. She didn't need them. She hadn't been exaggerating when she'd said she never had guests. But she wouldn't admit that to princy.

Shey stomped up the stairs to her room and took the bedspread and one of the three pillows off her own bed, then carried them back downstairs.

He had completely unbuttoned his shirt, but still had it on. Shey was grateful for that.

Yes, the feeling that washed through her was thankfulness, though surprisingly it felt a bit more like disappointment. Who'd have thought those two distinctly different emotions could feel so similar?

"Here," she said, holding out the bedding.

Tanner bowed at the waist and said, "Thank you," then took them.

She couldn't go without one more try to make him see reason. "Being my shadow is a waste of time."

"Ah, but it's my time to waste."

Tanner lay on the leather couch wrapped in the blanket Shey had brought. His head rested on the pillow.

Both smelled like her. Warm and spicy.

No sweet cloying scent for Shey.

He smiled.

Shey Carlson was an exceptional woman.

Captivating, even.

He chuckled as he thought about her attempts to get rid of him.

She was tough. She protected her friends with a ferocity that he couldn't help but admire.

Tanner was used to softer women.

Shey was all warrior.

He rolled again, trying to find a comfortable position, but the movement simply intensified Shey's scent. It was playing on his senses—surrounding him.

Tanner gave up trying to sleep and resigned himself to a sleepless night.

Here he was in a strange city—a strange country—sleeping on a stranger's couch. And his fiancée was less than enthused by his visit. He'd hoped when he saw her that he'd feel the magic, he'd feel some spark that would reassure him that they could make a go of marriage.

Instead he'd felt…nothing. Nothing but the remnants of a childhood friendship.

No lightning strike of passion.

No small blaze of interest.

Not even the tiniest ember.

After his disastrous relationship with Stephana, he'd seen the wisdom in his father's arrangements. Tanner felt that he wouldn't ever truly know if a woman loved him and not his money and titles, so why not marry a woman who had enough of each not to be after his?

In the end, Stephana had decided all the money in the world wasn't worth the hassles of noblesse oblige, the obligations of nobility. She claimed she hadn't signed on to be an unpaid workhorse. She wanted to party, to spend Tanner's money. When she saw that wasn't what she was signing up for, she left.

He didn't miss her. And he was honest enough with himself to know that not missing Stephana meant he'd never really loved her. Whatever he'd had with her, it had been a fraud on both their parts.

He and Parker would at least have honesty between them.

But no spark.

He snuggled farther into the pillow and Shey's scent surrounded him and he felt a surge of something.

More than an ember.

More than a small blaze.

It was definitely in the lightning category. A lightning strike of interest.

Unfortunately, she wasn't the least bit interested in him. And she was the best friend of the woman he should be thinking about.

Tanner dozed, and as he slept, he dreamed. Not of Parker, but of Shey. He dreamt of riding the Harley with her, holding her tight as feelings so intense that they threatened to burn him alive assailed him.

Shey was up before her alarm rang. It wasn't difficult, since she'd hardly slept. Knowing there was a prince in her living room had played havoc on her dreams, and those dreams had left her reluctant to go back to sleep. So she'd tossed and turned, dozing and dreaming, then fighting to stay awake and not dream, all night.

She hurried to get ready for work. If she was lucky, she would be long gone before Tanner woke up. She just needed a little distance from the decidedly handsome man to regain her equilibrium.

Tanner was off-limits. Not because he thought he

was Parker's fiancé. Parker declared that relationship null and void, so there were no worries there.

No, he was off-limits because even though there was some sort of chemical reaction when he'd wrapped his arms around her, that wasn't enough. He was a prince. A man used to the finer things. A man of social position and power. The finest thing in Shey's life was her business and her Harley…and of course, her friends. Though she liked her life just fine, she wasn't in the prince's league, no matter what sort of spark she felt.

She was grinning as she tiptoed across the kitchen. She was going to bypass the living room and sneak out the back.

She quietly turned the deadbolt.

She was home free.

She shut the door softly behind her.

"Good morning, Shey." The prince was leaning against her bike.

Darn.

"What are you doing out here?" she asked, glaring at him.

He looked way too good for a man who was wearing yesterday's suit and hadn't even shaved.

As a matter of fact, the stubble on his face took the sheen off his clean-guy image and made him even more attractive in Shey's estimation.

Not that she was attracted.

Not at all.

"I'm out here waiting for you," he said with a smile. "So, what's on the schedule today? Any chance we're going to see Parker?"

She noticed he'd given up trying to call her friend Marie Anna. Maybe she was making a bit of progress in convincing Tanner that Parker wasn't who he thought she was, that she wasn't the woman for him.

"No, we're not going to see Parker. I'm going to work and you're going to call your goons and do whatever it is a prince does to fill his days."

"Wrong. If you're going back to Monarch's, I guess I'm going to Monarch's, as well."

"Why don't you just admit defeat and go home?"

"I swore I'd bring a fiancée back with me, and I plan on doing just that."

"A wise man knows when the battle's lost."

"And a great commander would tell you that this particular battle hasn't even begun."

"Oh, shut up and climb on the 'vehicle.'" She sneered the last word in an attempt to mock him.

The prince was far too dense to recognize a good mocking. He just laughed and said, "Having ridden it yesterday I agree, a Harley isn't just a vehicle. It's a way of life."

Now *he* was mocking *her.*

Shey glared at him and stalked to the bike. She put her helmet on with a bit more force than necessary.

"If you're coming, get on."

"Any chance we can swing by the hotel first so I can grab a shower and change? You were sneaking out early, so I assume we have time."

"Well, if I'm stuck with you today I might as well make sure you smell good. Fine."

"You're a truly gracious host."

"I'm not a host. I'm your keeper."

"I have always been a man who resented being kept, being trailed by guards, having my every movement shadowed. But this once, I'm finding I don't mind it at all."

"You're perverse."

"Maybe, or maybe it's just…"

Whatever he was going to say was lost in the roar of the Harley. Shey kick-started it and threw it into gear.

Tanner surveyed the small dining area in Monarch's. Everything was neat and clean.

He felt a warm rush of pride.

Or maybe that warm feeling was merely the wet area of his shirt where he'd sloshed water on it when he'd rinsed the last load of dishes.

Either way, the day hadn't gone the way he'd thought it would.

He'd thought he was in control when he'd outwitted Shey and was waiting for her by her motorbike. He'd even felt rather triumphant when she'd taken him to his hotel so he could shower and change while she waited in the lobby.

But she'd thrown the first kink in his plans when she'd tossed a towel at him and taunted, "I don't suppose a prince such as yourself has ever had to clear his own table, but I'm thinking you're bright enough to figure it out."

She shot him a grin that said she doubted he was, in fact, bright enough.

That taunting smile should have made him angry.

Instead, it made him wonder what it would be like to kiss her.

A highly inappropriate thought.

So, he'd ignored the fact that when she smiled she stirred up embers of feelings best forgotten and taken her challenge to heart. That's why it was dinnertime and he'd not only mastered the fine art of bussing tables, but had also learned to run the monstrous dishwasher, and work the cash register.

He still had a tendency to splash himself when he used the nozzle to rinse the dishes, which is why his shirt was damp, but otherwise, he'd had a productive day.

Productive at least from the busboy end of things.

In terms of the prince finding his fiancée, he hadn't been nearly as successful.

"Hey, if the ruling-a-country thing doesn't work out, you might just have a career in the food industry," Shey said as she joined him. "You surprise me, princy. I thought you'd sit around and mope all day, but you really pitched in and helped. Thanks."

"A prince doesn't mope. And believe it or not, I've put in a hard day's labor in the past."

"Right. Signing royal decrees and proclamations can give a guy writer's cramp."

"Do you work at being abrasive, or does it just come naturally?"

"What can I say?" she said with a shrug and a smile. "It's a gift."

He couldn't help but smile in return. He could trade barbs with Shey all day. He rather enjoyed her prickly nature. Most of the women he'd dated in the past had bent over backwards to be agreeable, hoping to snag a rich prince.

He was pretty sure that Shey didn't have an agreeable bone in her body. If he said *black,* she'd say *white* just to have a good argument.

He glanced at his watch. He'd been here all day. "When does Parker arrive?"

"Oh, didn't I mention," Shey said slowly, "that today was her day off? Tammy's here to close up shop."

She grinned, obviously she'd had this planned all along.

A moment before, sparring with Shey had delighted Tanner, now it had him gritting his teeth as he said, "No, you didn't."

"So sorry. But today is Parker's day off. Guess you wasted time helping out here, didn't you?"

She looked completely pleased with herself.

"You let me slave away all day on purpose, knowing she wasn't coming in?"

"What part of 'I'm Parker's friend and would do anything for her' did you miss? That *doing anything* includes putting up with you all day."

He glared at the redhead. Somewhere along the line he'd lost sight of his ultimate goal and lost a whole day.

Now what?

Shooting an evil glance at Shey, he pulled out his mobile and called Emil to ask him to bring a car to the coffeehouse.

"You're giving in?" Shey said. "Wish I could say I'd miss you, but I don't tell lies."

"Never?" he asked.

"Never."

"I don't either. So if I said that despite the fact you're a highly annoying woman, I've been thinking about kissing you all day and that I find you to be a very attractive woman, what would you say?"

Tanner heard the words spill out of his mouth. He couldn't seem to stop them. He waited, expecting some sort of outburst from Shey, sure she'd take offense.

Instead, she laughed and said, "I'd say you wouldn't be the first to think I'm annoying, and you're also not the first to think about kissing me, or to think I was attractive. I'm sure you won't be the last to think any of them. But I'd add, I'm not interested in kissing you, although you're more than welcome to continue thinking I'm annoying and attractive."

"And what if I said that I don't believe the not-wanting-to-kiss-me part of your little speech? That I felt your eyes on me all day."

"I'd say, quite truthfully, that you were right. My eyes were on you. You know the old adage about not trusting a fox in the henhouse? Well…" She let the sentence hang.

"I'm familiar enough with American slang to know that you thinking I'm a fox could easily lead you to fantasize about kissing me."

She didn't even bother to respond. She just snorted and laughed again.

Tanner was thankful he'd never had problems with low self-esteem or else that snort might have put a dent in his psyche.

"I don't know why I bother," he said, shaking his head. "You're easily the most infuriating woman I've ever met. And if you knew the last woman I dated you'd realize that's saying something. So, as much as this has been interesting," he said with just the proper sneer added to the word *interesting,* "I'll have to say goodbye."

She wasn't laughing or snorting now. She suddenly looked all serious. "You're still going after Parker, aren't you?"

"Maybe," he said with a shrug.

"Then I'm going with you," she said, throwing down her dish towel like some cotton gauntlet. "Tammy, I'm leaving now."

"No, you're not," Tanner said.

"No problem," the young student said. "It was nice meeting you, sir."

Shey gave a quick wave to the girl and smiled at Tanner. "Yes, I am going with you. You owe me."

"How did you reach that misguided conclusion?"

"I not only met you at the airport, but I let you stay at my house. I even gave you the pillow and blanket off my own bed."

Ah. That explained why her scent was so strong.

"So now I'm cashing in. I'm coming along."

"Fine."

He tried to sound disappointed, but for some reason, he wasn't.

"Where are we going?" she asked.

"It's a surprise."

Chapter Three

"This isn't much of a surprise," Shey muttered as she sat in Tanner's living room. "It is decadent, though. I mean, most people stay in a hotel and are lucky to get cable TV. You've got an entire floor. I mean, this suite is bigger than my whole house."

"I've been to your house. It doesn't take much to be bigger." He'd hoped to get some reaction and wasn't disappointed.

She scowled at him. "Aren't you supposed to be hunting down Parker? I figured that's where we were headed. Are you calling it quits?" she asked, a hopeful note in her voice.

"I thought about starting a serious search, but after

the grueling day I spent working for a tyrannical boss today, I need a break and a decent meal," he explained.

Shey was right, he should be hunting Parker. The sooner he found her, the sooner he could convince her a union between them was a good idea.

But he couldn't work up much enthusiasm for going after his reluctant fiancée. He wasn't sure why, but was sure he'd be fine after a night off.

"Great, if you're not going to be chasing after her tonight, I can go," Shey said, sounding entirely too happy at the prospect.

Tanner should probably have just let her go, but he couldn't resist taunting her a bit.

"Ah, but you don't know. Maybe after dinner I'll feel like starting the search again."

Shey sighed and then lapsed into silence, sitting on the sofa, staring out the window.

The hotel suite had a great view of the bay, but he wasn't sure she was actually enjoying watching the lights bob on its dark waters.

He wondered what she was thinking.

Emil, Peter and Tonio were in the next room playing poker. They'd asked Tanner to join in, but he wasn't in the mood.

He was stewing over Parker. Tomorrow he'd just find her and convince her to come home with him.

Leave it to a woman to make a simple task so difficult.

This union made perfect sense. If he could really talk to Parker he was sure he could make her see that.

She'd grown up in the public eye. He remembered her teenage mishaps, and the way that the paparazzi had exploited her. As far as he was concerned, that was just another advantage to forging a relationship with Parker. She had experienced the worst aspects of living in the public eye, and therefore would understand what her life as his wife would be like. Always watched and measured.

And, despite being tabloid fodder, he knew she also understood what family meant. And a family was what Tanner wanted. One small sliver of normalcy in the midst of an abnormal existence.

He'd visited Eliason when he was younger. Parker's parents had been so different from his own. Her father might run a country, but anyone who saw King Paul with his children, knew where his heart was. Parker's parents had done their best to see that she and her brother, Michael, grew up as normal as possible.

That's why he had finally decided to agree with his father's plans.

He wanted a family...like Parker's. Something as far removed from his own cold, stark upbringing as possible. He'd given up on finding love, but maybe, just maybe, finding someone whose social background matched his, who believed in the strength of family, and understood the balancing act between a public and a private life—maybe he could find a family.

Parker was the most logical choice. And an added bonus was their childhood friendship. It gave them a starting point for something more.

It might not be a love-match, but he believed their similarities, shared background and friendship could be built upon. With enough building, maybe they would find love.

That's why he had finally decided to agree with his father's plans.

"My house is plenty big enough," Shey said, interrupting his musings.

"Your house?" he asked, then remembered his crack.

"Parker assures me that castles aren't all they're cracked up to be," Shey muttered.

He realized what he'd meant as one of the sparring digs had actually hit her. "I'm sorry. And Parker's right. Castles aren't always preferable."

"She doesn't want to go back with you...or without you, for that matter. She likes it here."

"Parker can run from it, but it doesn't alter the fact, she's a princess. She belongs with her own kind—with me."

"But in the end, going back would make her miserable. Marrying a man she doesn't love would break her heart. I can't let that happen. So, you're stuck with me until you decide to leave."

"Maybe, just maybe, being stuck with you isn't so bad," Tanner murmured, surprised to find he meant it.

Being stuck with Shey Carlson was surprisingly easy to get used to.

She shook off whatever mood she'd been in and started to laugh. "No, it isn't so bad…it's worse. I'm here to be your worst nightmare."

"I guess we'll just see about that," he challenged.

"Right now, if you don't mind, or even if you do, I think I'll go see if your goons will let me sit in on a hand or two of cards."

She didn't wait for him to answer.

Tanner watched her breeze into the other room, and, within minutes, she was ensconced.

Part of him wanted to go join the group, not because he had some overwhelming desire to play poker, but because that's where Shey was.

As the game went on, she became more and more relaxed with his guards.

"Straight," she said, pulling the pot of chips in front of her. "It's like shooting fish in a barrel," she quipped, laughing.

"Fish in a barrel?" Emil asked.

Shey launched into an explanation of the term as they dealt the next hand.

"Are you married?" Peter asked. He had his back to Tanner, but Tanner didn't need to see him to know he had that I'm-hoping-you-say-no expression on his face.

"No, and I don't plan to be."

"What a shame. A beautiful woman like you should be married," Tonio said.

Tonio? Now that was new. Peter was generally the flirt. Tonio was a quiet, serious man. Despite his size and abilities, he was normally shy around women. But obviously not around Shey. He continued, "…and have plenty of babies."

Shey laughed. "I don't think there's a husband, babies or a white picket fence in my future. I like my life exactly as it is. Serious relationships tend to complicate things."

"How about unserious ones?" Peter asked.

"Ah, now those I don't mind," Shey replied.

Flirting. She was flirting right back. With Peter.

Tanner realized he'd had enough. He rose and entered the second room. "I think the poker game is over."

The men started to clear the table, but Shey simply glared at him. "Pardon?"

"I said, that's enough cards for the night, Shey. My men have a full day ahead of them tomorrow. They're going to locate my erstwhile fiancée."

At the mention of Parker, Shey glared at him, even as she rose. "Thanks for the cards, guys. It was the best time I've had all day." She paused, shot him an evil look and added, "In a couple of days."

The men all bade their good-nights, and, shooting Tanner questioning looks, left for their rooms.

"Well, Mr. Party Pooper, that was nice. Just because you're pouting because you haven't spent your time finding Parker doesn't mean you need to make all of us miserable, as well."

"Maybe I just thought…how does the phrase go?" He dug through his memories of his college days in Boston and hit the right one. "Turnabout is fair play."

Thinking about Boston brought so many memories back. He'd spent four years in Cambridge at Harvard. Four years in relative anonymity. A small taste of freedom in the midst of a restrained life.

Shey reminded him of that time. Brash, free, exciting.

She was a breath of fresh air that made him wonder just when it was he forgot how to breathe.

He remembered riding into Erie on the back of her bike, pressed to her, holding her. She was an attractive woman, who didn't seem to realize it. He thought about being tucked on her couch, surrounded by her scent, knowing she was upstairs.

Now, watching her flirt with his man. Yes, she made him miserable, all right.

Rather than tell her any of that, he said, "Let's just say you're not making me happy."

Shey also reminded him that when he'd left Boston he'd left that part of him—that freedom—behind…a part that Shey exemplified.

Yes, she definitely wasn't making him happy.

Shey grinned and replied, "Well, then I guess I'm doing my job."

"Are you comfortable?" Tanner asked, still formal and almost pensive.

They were the first words he'd said to her since her doing-her-job comment. She'd meant it as a joke, just another one of their jabs, but it seemed to have bothered him.

Yes, annoying him, forcing him to give up and leave Erie without Parker was her goal, but his retreat disturbed her.

Before she'd entered the bathroom, he'd silently handed her a silky pair of pajamas. She didn't exactly swim in them, but they were big. But as she slid the soft fabric over her body, she didn't mind. It felt decadent and made her feel sexy. Shey was more at home in denim and leather, but, she secretly admitted to herself, maybe she should invest in some silk.

Silk underwear might work. After all, no one except herself would know she was wearing it, so it wouldn't mess with her image.

And for some reason, now more than ever, keeping her tough facade in place was a necessity. If princy saw any chink in her armor, who knew what he might do? Her first job was to keep him distracted and away from Parker. Her second was to convince him to go home alone…with no fiancé.

She had to admit, the day hadn't been as bad as she'd thought it would be. Tanner was a hard worker, and she'd actually enjoyed the poker game. Tanner's guards weren't as goonish as she'd suspected. Emil, Tonio and Peter were actually pleasant company. An added bonus was that they made a nice buffer between her and the prince.

Peter had spent the better part of the game flirting with her. She didn't take it personally. Peter struck her as the kind of man who had perfected these skills with lots and lots of practice. She found it impossible to hold it against the good-natured guard.

Emil was just fun. He had a deep, infectious laugh, and a quick smile.

And Tonio. He was quiet and serious compared to the other two, but by the end of the game, he'd started to loosen up. Until Tanner kicked them all out.

Shey didn't want to leave the bathroom and face

the prince. She wished she could just go home, but was afraid he'd be true to his word and go after Parker the moment she left.

Taking a deep breath, she walked out to the living room.

Tanner was standing by the couch that she had claimed for a bed, staring at her in a strange way. She looked down, and was reassured that the pajamas were as big as she'd thought they were. So big in fact that it was impossible to tell she had breasts.

So, this wasn't a he's-checking-me-out-in-silk-pajamas look; it was just another one of his weird looks, which he'd been shooting in her direction all day.

At first, they'd sort of set her teeth on edge, but at the moment she suspected any edginess she felt wasn't annoyance.

She wasn't sure what it was, but she felt suddenly warm.

"What?" she said.

"I *asked* if you were going to be comfortable." His voice was odd. Sort of a husky whispered quality she hadn't noticed before.

She walked past him and sat on the couch as she replied, "I'm sure I'd be quite comfortable if you'd stop staring at me like that."

"So my staring makes you uncomfortable?" he

asked, kneeling down so he was eye-level with her, a smile playing on his lips.

Shey would never admit it, but Tanner had a great smile. It didn't just play along his mouth, but traveled right up to his eyes, making them sort of glow with pleasure.

Pleasure?

She sure didn't want staring at her to bring him anything even remotely like pleasure. "I'm not going to play word games with you. It's late. Go to bed."

"Speaking of beds, you're welcome to mine," he said with a mock-leer while sort of wiggling his eyebrows.

Shey couldn't help a small chuckle as she said, "Sorry, princy, but I think I'll pass."

"Party pooper," he said, using the term she'd used on him earlier. He rose and started to walk toward his room.

"Tanner?" Shey called.

"Yes?" he turned.

Shey surprised herself by asking, "Do you miss her?"

"Who?"

"That woman you mentioned. The last one you dated, who isn't as infuriating as I am. Do you miss her? Miss having someone? I guess it must be hard to meet women in your line of work. Well, not exactly hard to meet women, but to meet ones who aren't after you for the wrong reasons. That was one of Parker's big fears—being wanted because of what she was rather than who she was."

"She told you that?"

"Not in so many words, but friends know these things. So, do you miss your last girlfriend?"

"No," he answered. "I should have ended it much sooner. The relationship was a mistake from the beginning. Stephana thought it would be all Cinderella on the dance floor at the ball, when in reality..." he paused.

"It's work," Shey filled in.

"Yes. And you're right about meeting women who see me, not the crown. I'm tired of women who want to play princess, who don't understand what the title truly means. That's why Parker is the perfect choice. She does understand what it means to be a princess, to live in the spotlight."

"She understands, and she doesn't want it."

Tanner shrugged. "As I said, there's my duty to my country. In Parker they'd get the perfect princess, someone who's already done the job, in fact. Stephana thought it meant money and luxury, when it is, as you said, hard work. It's travel, meetings, ceremonies you're always 'on'—always engaged with whomever you meet, wherever you visit. There's philanthropy, diplomacy, history and yes, even producing an heir."

"And you'd get a safe relationship. No more putting yourself on the line, taking risks on women who will never see anything but your title and your crown."

"Yes," he said. "So, you'll help me?"

"I'd like to say yes. I mean, I understand you a little better, but I still don't agree. Because even if Parker were the best thing that could happen to you, I don't think you're necessarily the best thing that could happen to her. She doesn't want to go back to that life."

"She was born to it," he insisted.

"But she's chosen a different way."

"Sometimes we're not given a choice."

"Right. But sometimes when we're not given something, we have to take it."

"What about you, Shey? Have you taken what you wanted, or simply taken what's been handed to you?"

"For me it's not a question of taking, but a question of working. I've worked for what I've got, worked my way to where I am."

"Was it worth it?"

She thought about Parker and Cara, about their friendship, about the businesses they'd built from the ground up. "Yes," she said. "It was."

Tanner studied her for a moment. Shey wasn't sure what she saw, but finally he smiled and gave a small nod. "Good night."

"Good night," she said.

As soon as he went into his room, she got up and hooked her keyring to the doorknob of the suite. If someone tried to open the door, her keys would clink, and, she hoped, that would be enough to wake her, because she had to get some sleep.

Who knew trailing after a prince could be so tricky?

Tanner glared at Shey the next afternoon. He'd thought they'd reached an understanding last night. But as she shot him a self-satisfied smile from across the small boat and waved, he wasn't so sure.

She was enjoying herself…at his expense.

She'd suggested that before he start looking for Parker in earnest they have breakfast on the bay. Her friend Cara had a boat and given Shey the key.

Tanner knew he should say no. They were on his turf, and he could easily use his men to keep Shey from following him. He could have made a clean break.

Instead, he found himself agreeing to breakfast and a water tour.

He should have known better than to trust her. Women were a tricky gender.

Of course, he was trickier. He touched the mobile phone in his jacket pocket and resisted a smile. Instead, he set out to distract her until the cavalry arrived.

"Fix it," he said, not for the first time. He didn't

need to point at the small engine at the back of the boat; she knew what he was talking about. She'd planned it, after all.

She kicked off her sandals, looked up and said, "Can't."

There was that smile again. It made his blood pressure spike every time she flashed that grin in his direction. He was sure the rush of heat that accompanied his increased heart rate was irritation. After all, what else could it be?

"You did something," he accused.

"Prove it." She turned and dangled her feet over the edge of the small motor boat looking totally relaxed...and sexy.

No, he immediately took that thought back. Not sexy. He couldn't allow himself to think that way.

"I don't have to prove it...I know it," he assured her.

He knew that she was sexy... No, not sexy. *Vexing* he quickly substituted, but not before his entire body tightened. She appeared so carefree, dipping her toes in the bay's water.

A small wave slapped against the boat and splashed her, but she didn't seem to mind that, either. She just turned toward him and said, "Ah, but knowing it and proving it are two very different things in a court of law. I don't know how it is in Amar, but here we're innocent until proven guilty."

"Shey, I think it's been a long time sihce you've been innocent." Even though he was annoyed, he'd meant it as a joke, but all hints of laughter evaporated from her voice. He'd like to think it was anger he saw in her face, but he suspected it was pain. He realized that he'd hurt her.

Tanner might have wanted to wring Shey's neck on more than one occasion since he'd met her, but he didn't want to hurt her.

"I didn't mean it that way," he said softly.

"Sure you did. I mean, a woman who rides a motorcycle and has a tattoo, who prefers her independence, why, she must have loose morals."

With sudden insight he knew that this wasn't the first time that Shey had felt stereotyped.

"That's not what I said."

"That's what you meant." She turned her back to him and slipped her feet into the water.

"What happened to innocent until proven guilty?" he asked. "I really didn't mean it that way."

"Okay."

Wanting to shift the mood he asked, "So what's your tattoo of?"

"None of your business," she said, definitely sounding a bit less upset.

"Where is it?" he asked. "I'll check for myself. Truly, I don't mind."

She turned back toward him. "I don't think so."

He thought he saw a hint of a smile and he felt heartened.

"Please?" he asked.

"Ah, I thought princes didn't ask for things, that they just gave orders."

"This prince doesn't just occasionally ask for things he wants, and I assure you that I also know how to apologize. For instance, right now I apologize for taking my teasing too far. You might ride a motorcycle, and even have a tattoo you won't disclose, but there's more to you than just those two tiny facets…they're not what I see when I look at you."

"What do you see?" she asked.

"A friend…the kind of friend who would do anything for those she cares about. Even going to the extent of following me around."

"For accuracy's sake I should probably point out that you followed me first. And that maybe you're not quite as obnoxious as I initially thought."

"I'd have to say that you're not quite as obnoxious as I thought, either."

"We'd better be careful…" she said with a full-blown smile now. "We're almost turning into a mutual admiration society."

"I don't know if *admiration* is the right word." Even as he said it he realized that the words weren't true.

He did admire Shey.

But there was more to his feelings for her than just admiration. He...liked her.

Liked. It didn't sound quite accurate, but it was close enough, he wasn't prepared to dig for a better description of his feelings.

He liked that she faced life on her own terms. He liked that she had no problem telling him precisely what she thought, that she stood up to him. He just liked the way he felt when he was with her.

Suddenly, even though he was in the middle of a wide-open expanse of bay and sky, he felt claustrophobic.

"So how long are you going to hold me hostage out here?" he asked.

"Maybe until you say you're ready to go back."

"Okay, let's go back to the hotel," he said, deliberately misunderstanding.

"No. Back to your country, to Amar."

He shook his head. "Not going to happen. You can't keep me out on this lake forever."

"No, but maybe I can manage to keep you here long enough for Parker to make her escape."

"What are we going to do to kill the time?"

"Enjoy the scenery," she suggested, grinning at him, sweeping her hand to encompass the shoreline.

Something in the middle of Tanner's stomach

twisted and he had a funny feeling that the scenery they'd each be enjoying would be quite different.

Tanner shot her a funny look, intense, as if he suddenly saw something Shey didn't necessarily want him to see. She felt a stab of nervousness.

"For instance," she said in an attempt to hide the fact he was affecting her, "this bay has downtown Erie on one side, and Presque Isle, a natural peninsula, on the other. You can go out to the peninsula and see some of the most beautiful sunsets ever. The beaches are great, and we have pontoon boats that take you on tours of the lagoons. It's a state park and there's a diverse array of animal and plant life, some of which you don't find anywhere in the area except on the peninsula."

"Maybe we could visit, I mean, if Cara's boat will cooperate and you're not planning to take me back to Erie anytime soon," he said, his eyes narrowing as he studied her.

"Oh, no, I'm much too smart for that," Shey said, laughing. "You're just hoping you can find a park ranger and report me for kidnapping."

"Did it ever occur to you that your description of the peninsula has simply inspired me to witness that natural wonder?" he asked.

"Didn't even cross my mind," she promised.

Shey enjoyed sparring with the prince. To be honest, she enjoyed his company. That was odd and she immediately decided not to reflect on why she enjoyed his company.

He'd be leaving soon, so it would be a moot point, anyway.

"Okay, so maybe it's not the scenery," he said. "Maybe I'm hoping if we go over to the beach you'll want to go swimming."

"Sorry, no swimming. We don't have any suits." They'd stopped at her house that morning and she'd showered and changed, but hadn't thought to grab a suit.

"I'll buy you a bikini." He wiggled his eyebrows in a suggestive, definitely non-royal way. He looked like a little boy, teasing her over who got the last cookie in the jar.

"Right," she said, with just the right amount of scoffing in her voice.

"I'd like to see you in a bikini." He wiggled his brows again.

Shey couldn't help it, she laughed. "It'll never happen, slick. I'm not a bikini kind of girl."

"Maybe you'd make an exception this once? I'd get to see your tattoo." He paused. "I would see your tattoo if you had a bikini on, wouldn't I?"

"Since I'm not going to put on a bikini, you'll

never know. Sorry to disappoint you. I mean, I realize a prince isn't used to being shut down, but princy, that bikini door is definitely shut."

"You're sure I can't convince you?"

"Positive," she said.

"There's nothing you'd bargain for?"

She thought a moment, then said, "Sure. You forget this foolishness about being engaged and leave Parker alone. If you do I'll not only tell you what my tattoo is, I'll show it to you."

Suddenly, the teasing evaporated. Tanner was all seriousness as he answered, "You know I can't do that."

"I know you *won't* do that. There's a difference."

"Stalemate, huh?" he asked softly.

"Yeah."

They floated quietly on the water for a few minutes. Shey kept stealing glances at Tanner. He seemed to be thinking hard about something. His expression was a study of concentration. He wasn't even noticing the beauty that surrounded them.

Shey loved it out here. She loved the smell of the water, the feel of the sun on her back, the sounds—

"I called for someone to pick me up," Tanner blurted out suddenly. "I have my mobile phone with me. My men are probably renting a boat now and are on their way."

"Then I guess we'd better give you that tour of the lagoons after all," Shey said.

She didn't want Tanner's men to find them because she was protecting Parker...nothing more, nothing less.

That's what she told herself. But the thought of Tanner leaving, of the day with him ending...well, it felt like disappointment. It was disappointment.

"We're going to hide?" he asked, not looking overly put-out at the notion.

"You've got it."

Chapter Four

She sat up with a start and checked her watch. It was getting late.

She looked at the still-dozing prince next to her.

After she'd called Parker on her own cell phone, she'd headed toward the lagoons, hoping to hide from Tanner's henchmen. It was one thing for them to find her in the open bay, but it would be much harder in the maze of lagoons that dotted the peninsula.

She and Tanner had been drifting near the edge of this particular lagoon for about a half hour. It was shady enough that she wasn't worried about a burn, and the day was warm and muggy, perfect napping weather.

She'd been napping all right, napping wrapped in a prince. He'd smelled…good. Fresh and clean.

Tempting.

And the last thing Shey needed was to be tempted by a crazy prince who thought he was engaged to her best friend.

"It's getting late," she said, nudging him. "Time to go."

He sat up, looking decidedly rumpled and bleary-eyed. "What do you mean late?"

"I know we've been having *fun* playing hide-and-seek with your gorillas, but it's time to go," she said with more than a subtle hint of sarcasm.

Truth be told, she had enjoyed the day. She couldn't remember the last time she'd taken a day off from work and done nothing.

Cara loved to take her small boat out to the lagoons and curl up with a good book. Her quiet friend had often suggested she give it a try, but Shey'd always declined.

She'd have to rethink that in the future.

"I have a meeting I can't miss," she told Tanner. "So it's time to call it a day."

"A date?" he asked, his eyes narrowing.

"A meeting," she said firmly.

"What sort of meeting?"

She toyed with the retort "Wouldn't you like to

know," but she realized how juvenile it would sound, so she worked to keep it in its place.

"I'll drop you off on the dock. I'm sure Curly, Moe or Larry would be happy to come get you."

She picked on his guards now more to needle him, not because she didn't like them. As a matter of fact, she'd enjoyed their poker game a lot last night.

Tanner didn't say anything more as she motored back to the bay and across its short expanse to the dock where Cara kept her boat.

Not one word.

No, he just stared at her, a slightly puzzled expression on his face.

She tied the boat up and stepped onto the dock.

"Well, it's been fun," she said, starting to inch away.

He still didn't say anything.

Oh, geez, the prince had had some sort of nervous breakdown on their trip.

What the heck was the word for nonresponsive people?

Catatonic?

That sounded close.

Rather than make her getaway, she walked back to the boat and climbed aboard. She walked right up to the prince.

"You okay? You've been acting weird the whole way back."

"I don't know," he said slowly.

"Don't know if you're weird, or if you're okay?"

He still didn't answer, just stared at her.

"I'm calling the goon squad," Shey said, sure she'd broken the prince. Did people go to jail for damaging royalty?

"They can't help me." His voice sounded a bit stronger—more with it—but he still was sort of off.

"Who can then?" Shey asked.

"You. Only you."

Before she could vocalize the very articulate *huh?* she was about to say, he pulled her onto his lap.

Shey started to squirm, trying to pull free, but then her eyes locked with his. His were dark brown eyes that bordered on black. Eyes that could hide things.

Shey wondered what was behind them. Who was this man?

She felt herself sinking into them, deeper and deeper. She was quickly lost in them, unable to pull away. She saw hunger.

And a wave of anticipation flared.

He wanted her. Tanner desired her, she could see it. He didn't try to hide it.

And she was sucker-punched by the realization that, though she didn't want to, she wanted him, as well.

She stopped struggling and inched closer, needing to bridge the gap of space that still separated them.

Her lips brushed against his, as light as the breeze blowing off the bay, a tentative caress that made her hunger for even more.

Shey had never been the type to wait for what she wanted, to weigh the implications of her actions. She was a jump-first, figure-it-out-later sort of woman. She went after what she wanted wholeheartedly, with no hesitation.

And right now she wanted more of Tanner's lips.

Forgetting he was a prince looking for a princess wife, she wrapped her arms around him and kissed him again, no hesitant introduction this time.

Her lips melded to his, parting slightly, inviting more.

Tanner groaned and gave her what she wanted, deepening the kiss.

Tasting.

Exploring.

Fanning the flames of her desire.

Making her want things that, suddenly, she remembered she couldn't have, shouldn't even want.

She pulled back.

"Sorry, I have to go," she said, jumping from his lap and hopping off the small boat without a backward glance.

Time to make her getaway.

Past time.

"See you later, princy," she called over her shoulder, hoping she had the same teasing lilt to her voice she normally did, but highly doubting it. The breathless quality made it tough.

"Bye, Shey. I'd like to say it's been nice, but I'm not sure it was. I *can* honestly say it has been interesting, though."

She didn't turn around and offer a "Same here," or any other parting words. Even though she always wanted the last word, this time, the only thing she wanted was distance between herself and Tanner.

See, that's the problem. She was thinking of him as Tanner now and not the prince.

She started walking toward the sidewalk, chanting a silent mantra—prince, prince, prince—to remind herself that this man, this royal pain in the butt was off limits, even though he was a knock-your-socks-off kind of kisser.

She passed her bike and kept on walking. She had about an hour before the meeting, so she wasn't in any rush. She could walk over to the library, then walk back later for her bike.

The walk would do her good.

Give her time to cool off and forget that she'd ever met Tanner—the prince.

The walk might even give her time to figure out exactly what she'd been thinking by kissing him.

Actually, answering that last question wouldn't take much time. She knew she hadn't been thinking at all or she'd have remembered all the reasons Prince Tanner Ericson was the last guy in the entire world she should be kissing.

She slowed her frantic gait until she wasn't exactly meandering, but was walking slower than her normal pace, going through the motions of enjoying the view along the Bayfront Highway.

She was pretty sure Parker was in hiding now. Shey'd done her best and certainly given her enough time.

Now she was done.

Dealing with the prince would be up to Parker. Her friend could either face up to him, or continue to dodge him. She could even let Cara take over babysitting him.

Either way, Shey was finished prince-sitting.

Prince-kissing.

Princing anything.

Suddenly Shey stopped. She felt she was being watched. And before she whirled around to check, she knew.

"Hi," Tanner said, smiling.

"What are you doing, Your Highness?" she asked surprised at how sharp her question sounded to her own ears. "I figured you'd already be in your limo by now."

"I'm following you," he admitted, looking utterly pleased with himself.

"This is ridiculous. You follow me, I follow you. Let's just say goodbye and stop the juvenile games." Suddenly she wasn't sure she understood the rules of whatever it was they were playing. But she was sure that at the end of the game she'd lose.

Shey hated losing.

"You're hiding something," Tanner said. "I haven't known you very long, but I could sense you didn't want me to know what you're up to, and I'll confess that makes me nervous. Just what sort of appointment do you have?"

"None of your business," she said, starting to walk briskly again. Unfortunately, his legs were longer and her brisk pace didn't leave him eating her dust. Now he walked comfortably by her side.

"Stop stalking me or else I'll call the cops. There are always a bunch of cops down here on the bayfront. They don't look kindly on stalkers."

"I'm pretty sure they would give me the benefit of the doubt. Being a prince has some benefits. Not many, but a few. And even if I wasn't visiting royalty, I can't help it that I'm walking in the same direction you are."

"Sure you can...turn around."

"No, I don't think I will. And if we do run across a cop I'll tell him who I am and that you've practically kidnapped me today."

"You're the most infuriating man I've ever met," she said, hoping she sounded more disgruntled than she felt, because she felt like laughing…like grinning ear-to-ear.

"I could return the compliment," he said, not looking any more annoyed than she felt.

"Fine." She shrugged, striving for nonchalance. "Come with me. What do I care."

"Where are we going?"

"The Blasco Memorial Library. It's just the other side of the dock."

"You have an appointment at a library?" he asked, sounding as if he didn't quite believe her.

"Every Saturday."

He waited for more of an explanation, not saying a word.

Shey sighed. "I meet with Lawrence."

"And just what do you and Lawrence do every Saturday?"

"It's a library…what do you think we do?" she countered. "I mean, you do have libraries in your country, right? Of course, as a prince you probably never had to use a public library. You just snap your fingers and Jeeves, your handy-dandy butler, brings you whatever you want."

"You're telling me you meet with this Lawrence to read?"

"Bingo."

"Let me get this straight. After kissing me like there's no tomorrow, you jump up, leave your Harley and walk a mile or so to the library to meet a man for a standing reading date?"

"Yep, that's about it."

"Explain," was his single-word command uttered in a princely sort of tone that probably was always obeyed by his minions.

Shey was pretty sure she didn't have a minionish bone in her body and she simply laughed at his attempt to command her. "Oh, don't go all princely on me. 'Explain. Bow down. Kiss my ring.' I'm not one of your subjects."

"Even if you were, I doubt you'd obey." There was a definite hint of frustration in his disgruntled tone.

"You got that right. I don't do obey well."

"What if I ask?" he said. "Shey, my sweet and helpful hostess, could you please explain why you meet a man every week at the library to read?"

She sighed a heavy put-upon sigh. "Lawrence was functionally illiterate. I mean, when we started he could write his name and make out some basic words, but reading a book, heck, reading the newspaper was beyond his ability. Everyone should be able to do more than just read to function, they should be able to read for the joy of it. We meet every week for him to practice reading, and if you insist on tracking me, I should tell you that I won't allow you to barge in and belittle him."

"You think I'd do that…belittle a man for trying to better himself?" Tanner asked, all joking put aside.

Shey knew she'd gone too far and shook her head. "No, I'm sorry. You wouldn't."

"Thanks for that much…at least."

"So, now you know," she said. "Go away."

"How about I just wait for you? Then I'll walk you back to your bike and you can give me a ride to the hotel."

"Aren't you the man that brought an entourage of employees along with you? Why not call on one of them?"

Tanner didn't want to admit that riding in a car with Emil, Tonio or Peter didn't hold the same appeal as riding behind Shey on the Harley.

So he just put his hands in his pockets. "I'm a prince. I do as I please, and it pleases me to wait."

He was pretty sure he heard muttering as she increased her speed and walked ahead of him—words such as *spoiled, annoying* and *idiot*—but he didn't mind. As a matter of fact, they made him grin.

"Then it's settled, I'll wait," he said as he caught up and once again matched his pace to hers.

"Whatever. Just leave Lawrence and me alone."

Those were the last words she spoke to him. When they reached the library she just waved him off and went off to find this Lawrence.

Tanner explored the library while he waited. And, of course, as he walked through the building he couldn't help passing by Shey and the man. They were seated at a small, private table in the back of the non-fiction department.

Lawrence was a slightly balding, paunchy man who had to be close to fifty. He and Shey were laughing at something.

She looked totally relaxed as she talked to him, all smiles and encouraging looks. But every time Tanner walked by, her smile evaporated.

He'd just wink and keep walking. He'd pretty much explored the entire library. It was built right on the bayfront and had great views. There was a maritime museum that adjoined it. He'd paid the slight fee and visited it, as well, and learned about the part the city had played in the War of 1812, including the role of the rebuilt brig *Niagara* that was housed in the museum. It wasn't there now. The brig toured during the summer, moving up and down the country's coast.

Tanner was back in the library when he suddenly tensed.

Shey was behind him.

He didn't need to see her to know. It wasn't even

that he could smell her light scent. He just *knew*. A feeling of certainty flooded his body.

"What was that all about?" she asked.

No, Shey Carlson wasn't one to ask—she demanded. She'd said he was royally bossy, but he met his match in Shey.

"All done?" he countered, not answering her question.

"Yes, not that it's any of your business." He had a feeling she was trying to sound testy, and he wouldn't be the one to tell her that she wasn't really succeeding.

"I'm going home now," she concluded. She turned and started toward the library's exit.

"So, we're sleeping at your place tonight?" he asked, easily keeping pace with her.

"No." She punctuated the single syllable with a glare. But again, it fell sort of flat—didn't have the annoyance level behind it that her earlier glares had had.

Tanner suspected, even if Shey would never admit it, that she didn't find him quite as much of an irritant anymore.

Just to try his luck, he said, "Oh, the hotel, then? Ah, I love it when women invite themselves to my room. Shows initiative. Makes a man feel wanted."

She didn't even respond this time, just glared at him harder. But if he wasn't mistaken, he thought he saw a hint of a smile playing at the corner of her lips.

"Now, Shey, we've only known each other a few nights, but I'm glad you can be so open with your wants and desires. And if you want me at my hotel, who am I to say no? Take me, I'm yours." He clapped his hands against his heart, thinking it made a rather dramatic addition to his speech.

"You're so funny. Too bad you've got a country to run. With an act like that you could have a real career in comedy."

"Maybe I should run away from my duties like your friend Parker and do stand-up?" he said. "I can see it now, Tanner, the Prince of Comedy could be my stage name."

"Right."

"Really," he said. "The idea of just giving up all the headaches and doing what I want could be truly appealing."

Yes, he could see the enticement of that. Knowing that people either liked him or didn't because of who he was, not because of what he was, of knowing that whatever he made of himself was because he worked at it, not because he was born to it.

"You can't do that and you know it," Shey said.

"Why not?" he asked. "Parker has."

"It's different, and you know it's different. Parker's got a brother who will take over the helm when the time comes. She said you were an only child. There's no one else."

"Actually, there are cousins who'd jump at the chance to take over. I'm not irreplaceable. Others could take over and I could pursue my career on the comedy circuit."

"You can joke around all you want, but we both know it's different."

"Because Parker's your friend," he stated more than asked.

Tanner had learned from the start that loyalty was part of Shey's makeup. Fierce, staunch loyalty. It was part of what he admired about her. And he was coming to understand that he did indeed admire this woman.

"I stand behind my friends, no matter what," she said, not really answering the question.

"Ah, you sound a bit disgruntled," Tanner pressed. "Does that mean you think Parker should come back?"

"Not back to you, but I've often thought that maybe she should be a bit more visible with her royalty. I mean, I can see how she could use her position to make some changes for good, not just in her country, but worldwide. Let's face it, people love royalty."

"I don't know about that," Tanner said. "I don't think my ex loves royalty at all."

"Maybe it's just you she doesn't like," Shey said. "And maybe I can understand that."

"Yeah, I'm sure you can." Tanner wouldn't have admitted it, but that one stung. He sped up, getting ahead of Shey.

She grabbed his arm and caught up. "I'm sorry. Trading barbs is one thing, I enjoy that. But I went too far and hurt you. I didn't mean to."

She looked so sincere that Tanner couldn't maintain his annoyance. "I think we've both crossed that line today. And you were right. I'm sure Stephana would assure you that she dislikes me as much as she disliked my duties as a prince of the realm."

"That's what I mean, your duties, your obligations. They give you a built-in audience, a platform to make a difference, to adopt reform."

"And that's what you think Parker could do?"

"No, to be honest, she's never wanted that type of power. But if I were a royal, that's what I'd do, use that position to speak about causes I'm passionate about."

"Like what?" he asked.

Shey didn't even pause to think. Her face lit up as she said, "Illiteracy, for one. There's an old saying that you can give a man a fish and he'll eat for a day, but if you teach him to fish, he'll eat for the rest of his life. I think they should add, if you teach him to read, he can learn not just about fishing, but about anything. Reading can take you anywhere, teach you just about anything."

He could see the passion in Shey and remembered that first night when he'd caught her feeding sandwiches to people from the back of the shop. "You'd like a platform to talk to people about feeding the person and their mind?"

She suddenly looked cautious. "No. I mean, can you imagine anyone listening to me like that? But Parker could command attention, and you could. You've both got the lineage, the whole royal thing to lend weight to your opinion."

"Being royal doesn't make someone's opinion and causes more worthwhile," he said gently.

"Let's just say that you have more power behind your opinion than a normal person, like me, would."

"There are many things I don't know, but one thing I'm sure of, you, Shey Carlson, are not normal."

"Nice," she said, a smile letting him know she hadn't really taken offense. "Really nice. Insult me after I've taken you under my wing. Making sure you were safe in this big, scary country."

He realized they'd both stopped walking. "Ah, so I don't need my bodyguards, I just need you?" he asked softly.

"There's not much I can't handle."

"I don't doubt it." And he meant it. "Speaking of handling, about the handling that happened earlier…."

Shey started walking again, her gait fast as if she could escape the memory.

"I don't know what you're talking about," she said.

"Sure you do. That kiss." Tanner knew no matter how fast either of them walked, no matter what they did, neither of them could run from the subtle change in their relationship that kiss had brought about.

And it was a kiss he'd like to repeat as soon as possible.

Problem was, he still felt guilty, even though his fiancée had told him she wasn't. And as much as he wanted to kiss Shey again, he knew he had things to work out with Parker first.

"I don't recall any kissing," Shey assured him.

"No?" Tanner asked, chuckling.

"No."

"Want me to remind you?" he asked, even though he knew he wouldn't—couldn't. At least not yet.

"No. There will be no more kissing."

"Suits me," he said, which earned him a nasty look that made him laugh again.

Even when Shey was annoyed with him, she made him feel a million times lighter than he normally did. Being with her, no matter what her mood, just felt good.

She treated him just as she treated everyone, like a normal man.

They walked for a few minutes in silence. Tanner

simply enjoyed her company. He noticed a lot of cars on the road, all heading toward one area near the marina.

"What's going on down there?" he asked.

"It's the amphitheater. They have outdoor concerts there all summer."

"Are they having one tonight?" he asked.

"Looks like it."

"Want to go check it out?"

"Don't you have to go stalk Parker?" she asked.

"Ah, sometimes it pays to be a prince. I don't have to do my own stalking, I have my men doing it for me. They're staking out her house, yours and Cara's. They'll let me know when she shows up."

"Cheater," Shey said. "Hiring people to stalk your stalkee isn't playing fair. But then, I guess a prince doesn't have to play fair. He doesn't have to share his toys or take turns or any of that kind of stuff."

Shey knew she should be miffed that he'd outmaneuvered her by sending his men after Parker, instead, she felt a small spurt of relief.

If Tanner's men were out chasing Parker then he wouldn't have to. And as much as she didn't want to admit it, she was having a good time with him—in an odd way.

"You certainly are an expert on royalty," he teased.

"I've been Parker's friend since our freshman year at Mercyhurst."

"And you're saying she doesn't play fair?"

"No, but we've already established that she's not a normal royal." She realized they'd passed the marina where her motorcycle was parked and were walking toward the amphitheater. "I didn't say I wanted to go to the concert."

"But you didn't say no, either. So I made an executive decision."

"You're being awfully heavy-handed," she informed him, but she smiled as she said it. Tanner was difficult and bossy—she should hate it—but really, she enjoyed it because it gave her a chance to flout his authority.

Shey knew herself well enough to know she'd always been, and would always be, a flouter.

"And you're being awfully difficult," he said echoing her description of him.

"Yes, it's a curse. I've always been accused of being difficult, although the term might not be all that accurate. It's just that I have opinions…opinions that are always right. People find that tough to swallow, so they label me difficult."

He laughed. "And modest."

"Yeah. Let's see, there's also stubborn and outspoken—"

He interrupted her. "I'm well acquainted with those aspects of your nature. But don't sell yourself short. There's also fiercely protective, loyal, funny, giving—"

"Okay, enough of that," she said feeling embarrassed. Those last few descriptions sounded like compliments rather than part of their verbal sparring.

"You don't like it when people see more than you want them to see," he said gently.

"I don't like it when people get the wrong ideas."

"So why don't you tell me what the right ideas are."

More kissing, she thought as she studied the handsome prince who'd proven he was a good opponent. And the fact that she was thinking about kissing prompted her to say, "The right idea would be to go away and leave Parker alone."

"Sorry, I can't go away just yet. Now, more than ever, it's imperative that we talk, that we settle things between us. So let's table the go-away conversation and find someplace to sit for the concert." He scanned the hill. "They don't have any benches?"

"Princes can't sit on the grass?" she asked, taunting him.

He didn't seem overly taunted. In fact, he just shot her one of those princely smiles that said he was used to humoring people and said, "Of course a prince can sit on the grass, but some prefer not to." He continued surveying the outdoor arena and finally said, "Wait here a moment."

Shey watched as he approached a couple, pulled out his wallet, handed them something. They handed him a plaid blanket.

"There," he said as he came back to her side. "Now we'll be more comfortable."

"You bought their blanket?"

"They had two," he said.

"You can't just buy someone's blanket."

"I believe I just did," he said, looking entirely too pleased with himself.

Every now and then Shey forget that Tanner was a prince.

For a while, it'd been easy to forget that he was different than her. But as he carried the plaid blanket down the hill, their differences were once again at the forefront of her thoughts.

She'd always had to make sacrifices for what she wanted. Put in the hours, kept her focus. The prince simply bought what he wanted. Just opened up his never-ending billfold and paid for it.

"You're quiet," he said, as he spread out the blanket. He extended his hand, as if she needed help to sit on the ground.

She ignored his hand and sat. Okay, not elegantly.

It was more of a plop. But she was down and she did it on her own.

"You're annoyed about something."

"No. Not annoyed."

"You would have preferred sitting on the ground than on a blanket?"

"No," she was forced to admit. "It's that I'm not used to wanting something and then just buying it."

"And I am?" he asked.

"Yes."

"And that annoys you?" He looked puzzled.

"No," Shey said, trying to analyze her feelings. "Not really annoys. It's that it reminds me we're different."

"I assure you that I've remembered we're different, and I must confess, those differences are what make the whole man and woman thing work."

"We're not a man and woman," she assured him, not liking where this train of thinking might lead.

"No?" he asked, quirking his eyebrow in a Mr. Spock manner.

"We are different, but not in the way you were referring to."

"Listen, Shey—"

"Shh. They're going to start."

"Hello, Erie," a woman shouted into the microphone.

The crowd roared as the band jumped right into its first song.

"I love music. I mean anything. From classical at the Philharmonic, to Jimmy Buffet," Shey told him. "They have a night every summer when a local band plays his songs. Looks like we lucked into it. Of course, I'm sure you spend your time listening to Mozart and Bach."

"I enjoy classical music on occasion, but I've been a Parrothead since college," Tanner said.

"Pardon?" she asked. Tanner, the Crown Prince of Amar, a Jimmy Buffet fan?

"You keep making assumptions about me," he said softly. "Assumptions about my life. Maybe it's time you stopped. You don't know anything about me."

"Except that you think you're here to marry my best friend and take her home."

"About that…" he started to say.

But Shey didn't want to hear about his plans for Parker, so she shushed him and concentrated on the music.

It was easy to let the tune carry her away to a place where water, wind and an occasional margarita could solve just about any problem.

She kicked off her shoes and leaned back on her elbows, just enjoying the lake breeze and losing herself in the sounds. But, all too soon the band was taking a break.

The noise of the crowd wasn't enough to cover the absence of the music.

"This is perfect," Tanner murmured.

"I don't know about perfect. It's been my experience that things can frequently be good, but never perfect."

He shot her an odd look, then slowly said, "I think you're wrong. I've witnessed perfection on more than one occasion."

"Such as?"

He didn't answer. Rather he just smiled and gave her a look that heated her blood.

"Stop that," she snapped.

"What?" he asked, assuming an air of innocence that didn't fool Shey for a moment.

His expression was soft and oh-so-kissable. And the smile that played on the edge of his lips only served to remind her of how good they'd felt pressed against hers.

"Stop looking at me like that," she said.

"You'll have to be more specific."

"Oh, why don't you go call your goon squad? I—"

Shey didn't get to finish her sentence. A sudden "yoo-hoo," interrupted her. She looked up and groaned.

"Problem?" Tanner asked.

"Not really, but just brace yourself."

"Shey, we thought that was you," two older women said in unison as they approached.

"You're right, it was," Shey said, plastering a smile

on her face when all she wanted to do was run...run fast for the hills.

"Aren't you going to introduce us to your man?" Mabel, Perry Square's acupuncturist asked.

"Yes, where are your manners?" asked Pearly Gates, whose résumé might say beautician, but who was in actuality the Square's know-it-all.

When Shey, Parker and Cara located their shops on Perry Square, they thought they'd merely found a quaint spot for their businesses. But in reality, they'd found a caring, tight-knit community—and Pearly Gates was at its heart. She was up on everything that happened on the Square, and what she didn't know, she found out.

Still, everyone loved Pearly and regularly visited her beauty parlor, across the square from Titles and Monarch's, for her sage advice and good old-fashioned wisdom. Everyone knew she had their best interests in mind.

"Sorry," Shey said, although she wasn't sorry about the lack of introductions, but rather that Mabel and Pearly had found her. "Mabel and Pearly, this is Tanner Ericson."

"Oh, this is him?" Pearly asked. "Parker's prince?"

"They know who I am?" Tanner asked Shey.

"They know everything," she whispered.

"You," Pearly said, her eyes narrowing. "You came

to steal Parker away from us. But it won't work. You see, you want her to be some hothouse lily, a flower that's cultivated and placed on show. But our Parker's a daisy, meant to blossom outdoors and free."

"I'm sure I don't see how this is any of your business," Tanner stated.

"Of course it's not our business," Pearly said with a laugh. "That's what makes getting into it so much fun."

"Shey, what are you doing out with this would-be thief?" Mabel asked.

"I'm not out with him, I'm watching him. There's a difference."

"There's a difference all right. And the difference is that I saw *him* watching *you* as we approached," Mabel announced.

Pearly nodded her agreement. "He was watching you, all right."

"What do you mean by that?" Shey asked.

"I mean," Pearly said slowly, as if Shey wasn't bright enough to pick it up otherwise, "there's a look in his eyes when he's watching you."

"We've all seen that look before," Mabel added. "Lately there's been an awful lot of that sort of look on the Square."

"But," Pearly said, "we're not sure we want a prince who's supposed to be looking at Parker the way he's looking at Shey."

"Pardon me, ladies. I'm sitting right here," Tanner said.

"What kind of look?" Shey asked, ignoring him.

"Like maybe he's thinking about kissing you...or maybe he *has* kissed you."

"Madam, I insist you give us our privacy," Tanner, suddenly all princy, declared.

Mabel laughed. "Oh, I should go back and get Josie and the rest of them...they'd love to hear this."

"They'd?" Shey asked.

"Oh, there's my date, Elmer, and Josie's Hoffman. And Libby and Josh are nearby with the kids, and..." Mabel trailed off a moment and said, "Come join us."

"No," Shey replied. "Tanner and I were just leaving."

"No, we weren't. And I'd love to meet your friends," he said. "But," he told Pearly and Mabel, "I'd prefer you didn't mention I was a prince."

"We won't," Pearly promised.

"Come on, you two." Mabel led the way.

Shey looked at the two older ladies, and the Cheshire-smiling Tanner.

She was trapped.

"Fine. But I'm not staying long. I've got to get home," she said, trying to lay down the law.

Not that anyone was listening. Tanner was walking with Mabel on one arm and Pearly on the other.

There was nothing for Shey to do but scoop up the blanket and follow them.

She had a growing sense that this was not a good move.

Chapter Five

"Hi, Shey," rang out from the small group as they approached.

Tanner glanced at the woman at his side, surprised that she seemed uncomfortable to be the focus of everyone's attention.

"I found Shey hiding out down the way and brought them along," Pearly announced. "This is her beau, Tanner."

"He's not my—" she started to protest, but Pearly just ramrodded on.

"Tanner, you know Mabel, and that's her date, Elmer. The one over there popping her gum is Josie and her beau, Hoffman. Let's see, Libby, Josh and their two rugrats, Meg and J.T. And that's Mac, Mia and their daughters, Katie and Merry. And—"

Pearly's introductions continued.

Tanner had been trained since birth to remember people and their names, but he was well and truly lost before she said, "And I think that's it for tonight. Normally Joe and Louisa would be here with their Aaron, but their newest addition, Ella, is a bit too young for outdoor concerts."

"Nice to meet you all," he said, sinking onto the blanket Shey had spread out.

"Now, about you and Shey—" the gray-haired woman started.

"Sorry, Pearly, but it looks as if the band's returning," Shey said, giving Tanner a look that said, "Don't say a word."

"Wait a minute," Josie blurted. "I recognize his name. Isn't Parker's fiancé-wannabe named Tanner?"

"And now he's dating Shey?" Hoffman asked, shooting Tanner a look that didn't bode well for his physical well-being.

"No, he's not Parker's anything," Shey assured the big-haired, bubble-blowing manicurist and her boyfriend.

"As to my relationship with Parker, that's a matter that would require a longer answer than I think we have time for," Tanner said in his most diplomatic tone. "But suffice to say, I don't feel that whatever Parker and I have will place any undue strain on my relationship with Shey."

Pearly gave him a hard look and then uttered a little harrumph. "I once knew a man who thought he could string two women along."

"What happened to him?" Tanner asked, surprised when the rest of the group groaned.

"Now he's done it," Mabel said to no one in particular.

"Done what?" Tanner asked Shey.

"Started her on a story." She shook her head. "You just couldn't be quiet, could you?"

"Well," Pearly continued, unfazed by the groaning and grumbling, "this man, Burkle Martellini, he was married to the banker's daughter, Ann. He worked in sales and was gone about half the week. Things seemed to go on well enough until we had a big county fair and Burkle took Ann. While they were there they bumped into…his other wife, Selina, from the next town over. Seems he was in sales—this Selina's father owned a brokerage firm. But the only traveling he did was about twenty-five miles down the road to this Selina's bed."

"What happened when the two women met?" Tanner asked.

"They had him arrested for bigamy, split his considerable bankroll and found they liked each other far more than they liked Burkle. Last time I was home they were still livin' together." Pearly paused. "And Burkle, he was sent upstate for a year. That's what happens to men who string women along—they end up in jail with a bunkmate named Bubba."

"I swear that in my country bigamy is frowned upon. As I said, my relationship—"

Shey elbowed him hard and said, "We don't have a relationship—with or without Parker in the picture."

Josie said, "Shh, the band's starting."

Tanner sank back on the blanket, ignored the dirty looks Shey kept sending in his direction, and concentrated on the music.

The setting was perfect. A warm breeze rolled off the bay, the sun was dipping behind the peninsula and Shey was sitting next to him.

Of course, she was sitting at the far end of the blanket, one more hitch over and she'd be on the grass. But hey, she was still sharing his blanket, and after the concert they'd be sharing her bike.

Tanner had decided that motorcycles were the premier form of transportation because they forced close proximity. Maybe he should amend that to motorcycles with Shey were the way to travel.

He inched a bit closer to her.

She glared at him.

So he moved even closer.

"Cut that out," she whispered.

"What?" he asked as innocently as he could manage.

She didn't reply, just gave him an evil-eyed look and watched the stage.

Just to egg her on, he put his hand over hers, sandwiching it between his palm and the blanket.

She tried to pull it away but he didn't release it.

"Let me go," she muttered.

"I'd prefer not to."

"It doesn't matter what you prefer. I'm not some serf in your kingdom who has to bow to your every whim and fantasy."

"Oh, you've been wondering about my fantasies, have you?" he asked. "If you like, I can fill you in."

"I don't like. You can just keep your fantasies and your hands to yourself."

Pearly leaned toward them. "You know what they say about love and war…it's a very thin line that divides the two."

An hour later, as the band bade their goodbyes to the audience, Shey made her farewells to everyone and took off at a brisk pace toward her bike.

She didn't look behind her to see if His Royal Toad was following. She hoped she'd lost him in the crowd, though she doubted she could be that lucky.

"Wait up," His Royal Painness called.

She didn't even break her stride.

"Are you mad at me?" Tanner asked, catching up to her.

"You enjoyed that," she accused.

The rat had liked letting everyone think there was something between them, rather than explain that the only reason she was around him was to save Parker from his attentions.

"Of course I did. Anyone in their right mind would enjoy good music in a lovely location, surrounded by fine people."

"You don't know any of them well enough to know if they're fine or not. And you're not going to be sticking around long enough to know them better. Don't you have a country to run or something?"

"Why are you so angry? It was nice to meet your friends. They were all delightful."

She didn't say anything. There was nothing to say.

The Perry Square crowd *was* delightful, but she didn't want Tanner to think that. She just wanted him to leave.

"Come on, so they thought we were a couple," he said. "It didn't hurt anyone."

"This is all some big joke to you, isn't it? Well, it's my life we're talking about. And I don't enjoy someone coming in mocking it."

"Mocking it?" he asked, looking truly puzzled.

"*Your friends were delightful.* I know you were comparing them to the people you associate with. A free concert outside doesn't begin to compare with the opera or some orchestra."

Tanner's puzzlement gave way to indignation. "So, now in addition to everything else, you're a mind reader and know what I'm thinking?"

Shey didn't have anything to say to that. If it were anyone else, she'd have apologized, but she should be happy Tanner was ticked off. Maybe he'd leave.

Just in case it might work, she said, "Go away."

"So tell me, oh Madam Soothsayer," he said, not going anywhere. "What am I thinking right now?"

"I don't know, and I don't care."

"I think you do know, and I think you do care. I think you care more than you want to admit."

Suddenly, she *did* know what he was thinking. Nothing psychic about it. She could see it in his eyes.

"Tanner," she said, hoping his name would sound like a warning, but afraid it was too soft to be taken as such.

Soft wasn't normally in her nature, but looking at him moving closer, she felt sort of melted, like an ice-cream cone in the afternoon sun.

"I don't think…" she started to say, but stopped because she couldn't think of what she didn't think. All she could seem to focus on was Tanner moving closer, as if in slow motion.

Closer.

Closer.

He paused for half a second before he kissed her.

She could have moved away, could have avoided his lips touching hers, but she didn't.

For a minute, she simply forgot everything except that he was a man and she was a woman, that this was what they were born to do. They were meant to stand toe to toe, wrap their arms around each other and kiss.

Destiny.

Their lips touched, a soft introduction. But it didn't take long for introduction to give way to knowing. Tanner knew what she wanted…no, what she needed.

There was no leader, but they moved as if they were of one mind, perfectly matching each other, move for move. Deepening the kiss. Shey could feel it flood her whole system. A kiss that started on her lips and spread to her toes.

Maybe that's where the term *kissed her socks off* came from, she thought.

Thought.

Thinking.

Quickly her brain kicked back into gear and she

realized she was standing in a parking lot kissing Tanner, surrounded by people. Strangers. Kissing a prince. Kissing a future king.

Kissing a man who thought he was engaged to her best friend.

She felt sick.

"I have to go," she sputtered.

"Shey, we need to talk about this."

"No, you need to call your men and have them give you a ride."

"You're going to just leave me here?" he asked.

"Yes. You're a big boy."

She got on her motorcycle. She'd never felt so relieved as she did when it roared to life.

"Goodbye, Tanner. I hope you have enough sense to realize there's nothing for you here in Erie. No fiancée, nothing. Go home."

Tanner watched Shey speed out of the parking lot. Her final words stung.

No fiancée.

He'd totally forgotten about Parker—again.

He realized that somewhere along the line he'd finally admitted to himself she was no fiancée, that Parker would never be his fiancée.

After Stephana, he'd assumed that was it for him, the end. As far as looking for love went, women only saw his crown. They fell for his position, his title. None of them, including Stephana, had ever seen him. And if he couldn't have love, he'd decided to choose a woman logically.

Parker seemed the perfect choice.

But since he'd met Shey—since he'd kissed her— he knew that logic didn't have a place when it came to desire.

He'd felt as much physical attraction to Parker as a man might feel for a sister. But Shey? She rocked him to his very core.

No, marrying logically, for practical reasons, would never work. At least not for him. And apparently not for Parker. She'd been smart enough to realize that before he had.

Tanner wanted more in a wife than someone who understood the demands of his life and his title. He wanted something more than just a good mother for his future children.

He wanted a woman who didn't care about his money or his title. A woman who wasn't intimidated by him and could hold her own in any situation.

He added to his mental list as he walked back toward his hotel.

A woman who had red, spiky hair.

A woman who knew how to laugh, knew how to enjoy life.

A woman who wasn't afraid of working for what she wanted.

A woman who drove a Harley and had a tattoo.

The moment they'd kissed, Shey Carlson had sealed her own fate.

Tanner knew with immediate clarity that he wanted her. He'd wanted things in the past that hadn't come to fruition, but this time he understood that wanting Shey was soon becoming something more. It was becoming a need. A physical and emotional pull that he couldn't deny.

Even *need* didn't seem an adequate definition.

He wasn't sure he could accurately describe how he felt, but he did want to explore his feelings for Shey.

In order to do that, he'd have to talk to Parker, to make sure that their engagement—one she'd never acknowledged—was well and truly not viable.

As soon as he was officially a free man, he was going after Shey.

She might put up a fight, actually, he was sure there was no *might* about it. Shey would fight him tooth and nail, but in the end he'd win her over.

He was confident of it.

"Parker?" Shey felt a surge of relief as her friend walked into Monarch's the next day looking none the worse for wear. The relief quickly gave way to guilt.

She'd kissed Parker's fiancé.

Okay, so Parker didn't think of herself as Tanner's intended. She'd done her best to avoid him. But still, Shey had kissed Tanner. A man definitely out of her league.

Cara walked through the doorway that connected the two stores. "Parker, where have you been?"

Parker looked a bit dazed.

"Parker?" Shey prompted.

"Tanner's been going crazy," Cara said. "His men have been all over the city looking for you."

Parker shrugged. "I don't have to answer to Tanner."

"We've been worried, as well," Cara said softly.

That seemed to shake Parker from her stupor. "I'm sorry I worried you two."

"I'm just glad you're all right," Shey said.

She gave Parker a small slug on the shoulder, then stuffed her hands into her pockets. She never knew how to handle emotional scenes.

"Do you have a way to reach Tanner?" Parker asked her out of the blue.

Parker wanted to get in touch with Tanner? What could that mean?

Shey nodded slowly. "I have his cell number."

"Great," Parker said, a smile of relief on her face. "Would you call him and tell him to meet me at my place at eleven. It's time we finished this."

Shey didn't want to talk to Tanner, but if Parker truly did set him straight, he'd leave Erie.

Her stomach twisted at the thought of him going.

The feeling had to be relief, because getting rid of Tanner Ericson was her goal.

"What are you doing between now and eleven?" she asked.

"I'm going to take a shower, get some coffee, and then call my father. Enough is enough," she said. "I'm done hiding, done running. I won't apologize for wanting to live life on my own terms, in my own way. Tanner doesn't have a fiancée. He's just going to have to face it. And my father? He can keep the money, keep my title. All I want is for him to love me for who I am. If he can't—"

"If he can't," Cara said, "then it's his loss. But I don't think you have to worry. Your father loves you. You love him. The two of you will find a way to work it out."

"Yeah." Shey felt sort of emotional and gave Parker another thump on the shoulder for good measure. "Good for you. I wondered how long it would take you to stop running away."

"Exactly this long, I guess," Parker said. "Because I'm done."

"Can we help?" Cara asked.

"No. I've got it under control. But thanks for asking. You both know how much you mean to me, right?" Parker looked as if she might cry.

Shey hoped she wouldn't. She never knew what to do when her friends were upset. She wasn't much at comforting. She knew her back-thumping didn't always have the desired soothing effect she wanted.

"And you mean just as much to us," Cara said.

"Yeah," she said, happy Cara had said it and all she had to do was agree.

"Good. You can get by without me at the store today?"

"We've got it under control," Shey assured her. "Shelly's coming back in. I think she's going to work out to be a real asset."

"I'm glad you didn't mind us hiring her without your approval," Parker said.

"I trust you two, you know that. Now get out of here and I'll call Tanner for you."

"Thanks again, Shey," Parker whispered, then walked out.

Cara hurried back over to the bookstore to shelve books before opening, and Shey stared at the phone.

She'd promised to call Tanner.

Why on earth hadn't she just given Parker the number and let her call him herself?

Because she was crazy, that's why.

She punched the number and breathed a sigh of relief when one of his men answered instead of Tanner. She was pretty sure it was Emil.

"Listen, tell the prince to meet Parker at her house at eleven."

"Who is calling?" he asked.

"Shey."

"Tanner said to wake him immediately if you called. He wants to talk to you."

"Forget it. I only called to deliver the message."

"But—" he started.

Shey hung up before he could continue his protest. The last man on earth she wanted to talk to was Tanner Ericson.

The phone rang, and her heart gave a weird little double beat. She squashed it down and tried to rake up a healthy dose of agitation as she picked up the receiver.

She lucked out. It wasn't Tanner. It was a very upset Jace O'Donnell, looking for Parker.

"...She didn't have a car here, didn't stick around for Belgian waffles," he told her.

Shey wasn't sure why making waffles for Parker was so important to Jace, but she wasn't going to tell him where her friend was. So she hedged, sure that if Parker wanted Jace to know where she was, he'd know. But she heard the pain in his voice and with a sudden insight realized that this wasn't about breakfast, or even that Jace O'Donnell looked at protecting Parker—the princess—as a job.

It was about the fact that Jace had feelings for Parker.

Parker and a private investigator? It made more sense than Parker and a prince. But Jace couldn't seem to get beyond Parker's princessness.

Shey could sense his conflict. He was worried he didn't have anything to offer Parker, and didn't seem to get that Parker didn't want diamonds and tiaras. The princess didn't want a Prince Charming to sweep her away.

Parker just wanted to be loved for herself.

Shey gently reminded Jace that her friend "…might have to play princess and snack on caviar and champagne on occasion, but Parker's a complete waffle girl. If you can't see that, then you shouldn't be making her any breakfasts."

There, she thought as she hung up, that had been subtle. She wondered if what she'd said got through to him?

It kept buzzing around in her mind. If a princess could have a private detective, could a regular woman have a chance with a prince?

No. Jace and Parker had far more in common than Shey and Tanner ever could. Because, although Shey might have enjoyed kissing Tanner, the truth was, she was a waffle kind of girl herself, and he was definitely all caviar. There was no middle ground when differences were that great.

To be honest, it really didn't matter. Once Parker gave Tanner the royal kiss-off, he'd be gone. And of course, Shey would be glad to see the last of him.

Yes, that sinking feeling in the pit of her stomach was simply an odd manifestation of her happiness.

Chapter Six

That evening Tanner watched as Shey told her new employee, Shelly, she could go home.

At last they'd be alone.

He'd been bursting with a sense of what was possible all day, wanting to tell Shey he was truly free of his delusional engagement.

His meeting with Parker had been rather straightforward. They'd both agreed that the engagement was a farce, that they were both clear of it and had parted on good terms.

He'd felt an unbelievable sense of relief as he left his childhood friend at her apartment. He'd been a fool to think that he'd ever be able to settle into an arranged relationship. What he wanted was something less formal. Something different. Something…someone like Shey Carlson.

He wasn't sure where a relationship with Shey would end, but he was sure it would be like that first ride on the back of her Harley. An exciting and invigorating ride into new, uncharted territories. With Shey at the wheel, it couldn't be anything but that.

The first step was asking her to go out with him on a real date.

But Shey had been avoiding him all day. There'd been no time for heart-to-heart talks. Now that Shelly was leaving, Shey would have to talk to him.

Peter, who had been milling around the shop all night, asked, "I'm going to take Shelly home, all right?"

"Sure," he said, even as Shelly said, "I can get home on my own."

Peter ignored the woman's protest and followed her out of the shop. He shot Tanner a quick wave and said, "Don't wait up for me."

Shey walked over to the door and flipped the sign to Closed.

"You can leave now, as well," she said, blunt and to the point.

"Oh, I don't mind waiting," he assured her.

She rolled her eyes and walked back behind the counter muttering. He caught words such as *prince,* and *pain*. It didn't take any great leap of intuition to fill in the blanks.

She opened the refrigerator and took out an assortment of items. Lunch meat, lettuce, mayonnaise. Then she opened up a loaf of bread and started making sandwiches.

"What are you doing?" he asked, suspecting she was stalling, trying to keep busy.

But it didn't matter. He'd wait. He felt light, as if breaking things off officially with Parker had set him free.

"Uh…" Shey looked embarrassed, like a child caught with her hand in the cookie jar. "I'm making some sandwiches for tomorrow."

"Wouldn't it be better to wait until morning and make them fresh?"

Rather than answer, she said, "Why don't you fill the salt shakers and sugars instead of watching me work and second-guessing my methods?"

Tanner, feeling fairly adept at the whole shop thing, obliged. But even as he worked, he watched her. When Shey had filled the tray with sandwiches, she lifted it and carried it into the back, rather than wrapping them and putting them in the front cooler.

Tanner was pretty sure he knew what she was doing, but cracked the door and watched, just to be sure.

She opened the back door, and sure enough, there was a small crowd waiting for her there.

"Leo," she said as the first person approached. "Did you sleep inside last night?"

"Sure did, Shey. My cough's almost gone." He helped himself to two sandwiches, stuffing one in his pocket and taking a bite of the other. "You make the best ham and cheese."

"I don't think it takes any special talent to take a piece of ham, cheese and add a bit of lettuce."

"It's your special sauce."

She chuckled. "Mayonnaise and mustard. Nothing special there."

She greeted the rest of them by name, chatting with them, laughing with them.

Silently, Tanner held the door ajar. He'd been touched the first time he'd witness her handing out leftovers from the day. But today had been crazy…busy.

There were no leftovers.

So she'd made more sandwiches.

Tanner felt something warm spread through his system. Shey. She was a most amazing woman.

The phone in his pocket rang its little chimes. He quickly stepped back and started to close the door to the kitchen, but not before Shey turned and saw him.

Their eyes met and held. And for that split second they were the only two people in the world.

The phone rang again, and the moment slipped by. Shey scowled, but Tanner wasn't fooled. It wasn't so much his presence, but that he'd caught her in the midst of an act of kindness. He didn't know Shey as well as he planned to, but he knew her well enough to realize that she wanted her many kindnesses to remain secret.

She tried to maintain her image as a tough-guy…girl. No, woman. Shey Carlson was all woman. A woman who tried to present a tough image, but who in reality was a soft touch.

The phone rang a third time.

Tanner dug it out of his pocket. "Yes."

"Just where are you now, boss?" Emil asked.

Shey stalked out of the kitchen and shot him a disgruntled look.

He couldn't help but smile, not the least bit intimidated.

"Boss?" Emil repeated.

"I'm fine," he replied, not really answering the question about his whereabouts.

"You're still tracking the princess? Want some help?"

"No. I caught up with the princess this afternoon and we've decided things aren't going to work between us. I'm officially unengaged." He caught Shey's eyes as she looked up at the words.

"So we're going home?" Emil asked. "It's about time. Between you and your chase, and now Peter's odd infatuation with some girl, things are out of control. It's time to go."

"No, we're not going home." Tanner's gaze held Shey's. "No, not quite yet."

"But if you're not going after the princess anymore then—" Emil cut himself off abruptly. "Oh."

"Would you care to explain that *oh?*" Tanner asked.

"No, I don't think I would." The guard laughed and said, "But if I were to make a guess, I'd say that the reason we're staying a little longer has red hair and plays a mean hand of poker."

"You do remember that I'm your employer, right? And that discretion is part of the job description?"

"Sure thing," Emil assured him, not a hint of being intimidated in his voice. "I did call you boss, after all."

Tanner was pretty sure that being called boss on occasion didn't necessarily mean anyone in fact remembered he was supposedly in charge.

"I gave Peter the night off, so don't wait up for him," Tanner told Emil.

"Wait up for Peter? I'm not that crazy. You know how he is."

Tanner thought about the way Peter had been acting around Shey's newest employee, Shelly. "I don't know," he said slowly. "Something seems different this time." He heard a distinct scoff on the other end of the phone. "Since I won't be back, you and Tonio have the night off."

"I don't know about Tonio, but I'm going to stay safely in the hotel so whatever is causing all this women-on-the-brain stuff doesn't affect me."

"I'll see you sometime tomorrow," Tanner concluded, then disconnected.

"You should have told him you'd be back soon," Shey said, obviously not the least bit embarrassed to practically admit she'd been eavesdropping.

Not that Tanner had tried very hard to keep his conversation private. He'd wanted her to hear the part about his never-quite-real engagement being officially over. She hadn't asked how his meeting with Parker had gone. Not that he expected her to.

"Maybe I was hoping you'd go out with me when we finished up here."

"Sorry. If you've finally admitted there's nothing between you and Parker, then my job's over."

She was trying to get rid of him, it didn't take a rocket scientist to figure that out. But he didn't think it would take her long to figure out that getting rid of him wasn't all that easy.

"Good," he said. "I don't want to be a job for you." He took a step toward her.

"What do you want?" Shey asked, ducking behind the counter, using it as a barrier between them.

"I think you know," he said, leaning toward her.

"Get that kissy look off your face," she snapped, stepping back so that the only way he could reach her would be to climb over the counter, or come around.

"There will be no more of that," she assured him.

"Why not?" he asked. "I'm officially a free man now. We're both young and single. There's definitely a spark between us. You know it's what we both want."

"There are a lot of things I might want, but don't allow myself to have. Too much fried food, for instance. I might enjoy it, but I avoid it. Gives me heartburn."

"Do you think there's something Freudian to comparing me to a burning heart?"

She shook her head. "You're impossible, and you're also a prince. A prince who's going home."

"I haven't decided when I'm going home. There are still a few sights in Erie I'd like to see. A few things I'd like to do."

"Fine. You'd best call your men and start seeing and doing them so you can leave."

"I'd rather see them and do them with you."

"I don't think so. There's no point. Now, if you don't mind—"

"Fine. I'll go for now, but I'll be back."

* * *

I'll be back, Tanner had said Sunday when he'd left Monarch's. And he had indeed followed through, coming back day after day, no matter how rude Shey tried to be.

As a matter of fact, the man seemed to thrive on her insults.

He came by Monarch's when she was working, offering to help. Shey refused.

That didn't stop him. He sat with his henchman, Peter, and became a day-long customer.

Come to think of it, Peter had pretty much made himself a fixture at the shop. At least, whenever Shelly Richer was working.

The newly divorced mother of two seemed as flustered by Peter's attentions as Shey felt over Tanner's. She truly didn't know what to do with the prince.

It got worse midweek when Tanner started sending flowers.

Flowers?

Shey had never thought of herself as a flower sort of woman. And although she scowled for Tanner's benefit, she liked that he'd figured out she wasn't the type to appreciate roses. Hothouse flowers didn't impress her. But the small arrangement of daises…well, if she was someone who liked flowers, she'd probably pick daisies. Something that grew wild, with little regard for the rules.

On Saturday she opened the store.

No flowers were waiting.

And no Tanner.

Well, that was good, she assured herself as she started the coffee and signed for her morning delivery of pastries from the bakery. Maybe Tanner had finally gotten the hint. She hadn't been subtle, after all.

She'd served the first customers and began loading up the display case when the bell over the door chimed. She looked up, expecting Tanner. And assured herself that was relief she felt when she saw it was Parker walking in the door.

Yes, that sinking feeling in her stomach had to be relief. The prince was finally out of her hair. He'd finally gotten her not-so-subtle hints.

"Hey," she said to Parker.

Parker grunted a response.

Parker wasn't much of a grunter—it wasn't really a princessy trait—so it wasn't hard to guess something was wrong.

"Bad day?" Shey asked.

"No, of course not," Parker replied. "I mean, if it was a bad day I'd simply call my daddy and tell him to make it better. I'm a princess, after all, and I get what I want."

"Parker?" Shey asked, wishing Cara was here. It was obvious that Parker was about to unload all sorts of emotional baggage stuff, and Cara was much better at handling that than she was.

Much, much better.

Shey studied Parker and concluded that whatever was bothering her friend had to do with a man. Jace? Probably. She knew that particular expression of annoyance on Parker. She'd probably worn it herself as she dealt with a certain irksome prince.

Though she wasn't sure what Jace had done, she knew Parker needed to vent. Again, she thought about calling Cara, who would certainly know the right words to say to calm Parker down. But before she could make her move, Parker whirled around and said, "Problems? What kind of problems could a princess like me possibly have? I'm spoiled. I have the world at my feet, my every desire within my grasp. All I have to do is wish it and make it so."

Yes, she'd been right—a man. She looked toward the doorway to the bookstore and wished Cara would suddenly appear. When Cara didn't appear, Shey tried to think of something comforting to say and finally settled for, "Men are more trouble than they're worth."

Parker took a deep breath and seemed to get herself under control. "Not all men, it appears. Judging from the flowers and his constant presence at the store whenever you're working, I'd say Tanner's proving worth it. Are you two having fun?"

"Fun? Ha," Shey scoffed. "Torture. The guy won't take no for an answer."

Except, he wasn't here, so maybe he had.

"Do you really want him to?" Parker asked softly.

"Of course I do. I mean, he's a prince. He's got more important problems than making me miserable."

Parker shook her head. "I don't know, Shey, he's been very persistent."

"He was persistent with you, and eventually he got the message and gave up. He'll get my message soon. Why, he's not here this morning, so maybe he's already got it."

"You know, that's the thing. He wasn't all that persistent about finding me. I mean, after you picked him up at the airport and we had that first confrontation, avoiding him wasn't all that hard." She studied Shey a moment and added, "Not hard at all."

"Because I was running interference," Shey said quickly, not sure she liked the way this conversation was turning. "Hey, have you given any thought to the new cappuccino machine?" she asked, hoping to get Parker off her current train of thought.

"Or," Parker said slowly, as she glanced at the

flowers Tanner had sent, "maybe Tanner wasn't all that persistent because he wasn't as convinced as he pretended to be that *us* was a good idea. He seems to be more convinced—more persistent—about you."

"I'm just a passing mental aberration, a substitute because you shut him down."

"Shey, you are many things, but a substitute for anyone isn't one of them. You're unique. Incredible. Tanner would be lucky if his pursuit paid off."

Shey stuffed her hands in her pockets and wondered what to say to that. She never knew what to make of compliments. They made her distinctly uncomfortable. So she ignored them altogether and simply zeroed in on the Tanner part. "I think he's done pursuing. He's not here now. That's a first. He's probably on his way back to Amar."

"I don't think so," Parker said.

"Well, I do. And it's just as…" Shey let the sentence trail off as the door to Monarch's opened and Tanner walked in, trailed by a guy with a violin.

A real violinist, carrying his violin in the crook of his neck and not in a case.

"Tanner," Shey said, her voice full of warning. Any sane person would hear her and be afraid—very afraid. But Tanner wasn't most people.

He smiled a very unprincely, got-ya sort of grin and said, "Shey, this is my friend David."

The man bowed, then stood, violin poised in the crook of his neck again.

"What do you and David want?"

"I'm here to ask you out on a real date. And since I know how you're apt to respond, David's here as moral support."

"No," she said.

She'd have to be out of her mind to go on a real date with Tanner. Look what happened when she was with him and not dating. An awful lot of kissing, that's what. And the last thing she needed was to risk more kissing…and more.

"Okay, David," Tanner said, "she asked for it."

The violinist started playing a slow, mournful tune.

"Stop that," Shey insisted. "Parker, help me get them out!"

Parker didn't answer, and Shey turned and found Parker hadn't answered because she couldn't—she was too busy laughing hysterically.

Cara came in from the bookstore and said loudly so as to be heard over the violin, "Shey, what are you doing?"

"I'm not doing anything. This guy—"

"David," Tanner supplied.

"David's doing it." She turned to the violinist. "Stop."

He just kept on playing.

"I hired him and he won't stop until I say so," Mr. I-can-buy-whatever-I-want said.

"What will it take for you to say so?" Shey asked, though she already knew.

"A date."

"Browbeating women into dating you isn't very princely. It's blackmail."

"Not really," Tanner said. "I mean, it could have been much worse. I was going to hire a hand-organist. That would have been blackmail."

"An accordion?" Shey said.

"Or a bagpiper," he said happily. "I think they're my next step. Have you ever been serenaded by the bagpipes? Maybe a whole band of bagpipes? It might be good for business."

"Tanner, this isn't funny." Shey felt an overwhelming need to stomp her foot again, and ignoring the feeling was harder than it should be. Tanner could try anyone's patience enough to need an occasional stomp.

"It's not funny at all," she repeated.

Parker's giggling sort of took away from that comment.

"Cut it out," she said to her friend. Parker didn't even try to stop. As a matter of fact, her laughter escalated.

"Come on, Tanner. I know you don't have to work

for a living, but this is my business. The customers don't want to deal with your nonsense."

"Sure we do," some helpful soul cried out.

Shey planned to find out who it was and make sure they got grounds in their next coffee. The early-morning crowd took their coffee very seriously.

"All you have to do is say yes," Tanner said, "and David and I'll be on our way. I'll pick you up for the date at about six."

"No," Shey said.

"I'm sorry to do this to you." He nodded at David, who stopped the sad tune and started a new, snappier piece.

"I like this one better," Shey said at the very same moment Tanner started singing.

Loudly.

Off-key.

It was the kind of singing that was so horrible that it was impossible to make out the words.

So horrible that any sane person with half an ear for music felt compelled to do anything to stop it. That had to be the reason Shey heard herself say, "Fine."

Tanner stopped his caterwauling and motioned to David the violinist, who also stopped.

"Say it again, in front of all these witnesses."

"Yes, I'll go out with you as long as you promise

no more singing…or violins." She thought about bag-pipes and accordions and added, "No musical in-struments in the coffeehouse."

"I promise," he said. The grin on his face took some of the sincerity away from the promise. "Six. I'll pick you up at your house at six sharp."

"Pick me up here," she said. No way was she let-ting him near her house again. He might want to stay over, and of course, that was the last thing in the world she wanted.

"See you at six, then," he said.

Then both men left and Shey groaned. "What on earth did I just do?"

She looked to her friends, her two best friends, for some support. But a poor-baby, and maybe even a let-us-help-you-plan-your-revenge seemed nowhere in sight. And Parker was especially good at getting revenge.

So Shey didn't get any of the sympathy she wanted. All she got was more laughter.

"Nice," Shey said, shaking her head in disgust. "Enjoy your jocularity. Just remember, what goes around comes around."

Parker had the grace to look nervous, but Cara just laughed. Maybe she thought because she wasn't em-broiled in some big-man brouhaha she was safe, but Shey knew better.

After all, Shey hadn't meant to be in this position with Tanner. All she'd wanted to do was run interference for a friend.

And now look where she was…about to go on a real date with a prince.

How on earth had things come to this?

Chapter Seven

Shey refused Cara and Parker's offers to help her dress for her date.

She refused to think of the evening as a date.

It was payola, plain and simple.

Just her way of getting the crazed prince out of her store. And after tonight she planned to have him out of her life, as well. He was probably planning to take her to some fancy-shmancy restaurant and wine and dine her until she lost all sense and kissed him again.

She'd show him.

She looked down at her faded blue jeans, her I Love Trouble T-shirt and her black leather jacket that was a bit too warm for a late-spring evening. She thought about taking the coat off, but it really was a necessary part of her ensemble, so she left it.

She felt like the antithesis of a woman a prince would date.

"That's what you're wearing?" Parker asked, sounding like a disapproving mother hen.

"Yep."

Parker shook her head. "There's still time to change into a different outfit."

"No way. I wouldn't be in this mess if I hadn't tried to save you from that crazy prince."

Parker didn't look the least bit contrite. "You might have started out trying to save me, but I don't think I was in the forefront of either of your thoughts for very long."

"Leave her alone, Parker," Cara instructed.

"See," Shey said, smiling at their friend. "Cara knows this outfit is guaranteed to chase all princes away."

"Cara knows nothing of the sort. That outfit will have Tanner drooling all over you." Parker looked her up and down, assessingly. "You're hot."

"You've got to be kidding. There's nothing sexy about this outfit. Heck, the T-shirt even tucks in. You can't see the slightest inch of skin."

"Sometimes," Cara, the bookseller-turned-fashion-consultant, said, "it's the things you can't see that are the most intriguing, the most sexy. You look biker-chic."

"Ha." Shey tried to sound confident, but felt a bit worried. She didn't feel chic, biker or otherwise. But maybe she should go change before—

As if on cue, Tanner, the way-too-prompt barnacle on the backside of her life, walked into the store.

"I see you're ready," he said, all smiles.

Smiling…that wasn't what she expected. "Don't you want to order me to go change?"

"Do you want to change?" he asked.

"Not particularly. I'm comfortable as is." But that was a lie. There was a gleam in Tanner's eye that left her feeling decidedly uncomfortable. She didn't believe she was exactly hot, but maybe Cara was right, maybe biker-chic wasn't the way to go.

"Well, the jacket might be a bit warm, but that's up to you." He opened the door. "Are you ready?"

There was a challenge in his tone, suggesting he doubted her readiness.

She forced her shoulders back, and met his eyes as she did her best to growl, "Yeah, whatever."

"Ah, your enthusiasm for this evening is overwhelming." He didn't look any more intimidated by her attempted growl than he did by her outfit.

"So where are we going?" she asked as he led her from Monarch's. "Some fancy restaurant where you can show off your whole princy thing and try to impress me? Well, guess again, bucko. It won't work."

"Guess again, yourself," he said. "I have other plans for our date."

"It doesn't matter. I only agreed to go out with you because you blackmailed me. It's not a real date if you have to force the girl to go out with you."

"But some women take a bit of creative encouragement. And I guess my creativity worked just fine because here we are." He looked completely pleased with himself.

Without another word he led her to the waiting limo.

Shey felt a moment of panic as she climbed into the lush interior.

Tonight was a mistake. She was sure of it.

"Bowling?" Shey asked again.

"Hey, I *bought* us shoes," he said. "I'm the kind of guy who spares no expense when I'm trying to woo a woman."

She glared and didn't reply.

"So is it working?"

She began to lace up her new bowling shoes with a little more force than was necessary. "Is what working?"

"The wooing."

She scoffed. But Tanner was pretty sure he saw a hint of amusement in her eyes.

He'd known that an ordinary wine-and-dine type of evening wouldn't work on Shey. And when he'd walked in and saw her outfit, he knew he was right. She was dressed to annoy. Unfortunately, annoyance wasn't his primary feeling when he saw her.

Desire.

It hit him like a ton of bricks. But it wasn't just the outfit, although her pink I Love Trouble T-shirt along with the black leather jacket looked more cute than ominous. Every time he saw Shey, the flood of desire struck.

He didn't even have to see her. Just thinking about her was enough.

"I just wanted to take you on an ordinary first date." Deciding what constituted an ordinary first date had been hard work. He couldn't think of anything that might impress her, so he'd settled for amusing her.

Despite her scowl, he was pretty sure he'd succeeded.

"I don't think renting out an entire bowling alley constitutes as ordinary." She had that same tone in her voice she used when complaining that he'd bought them a blanket.

"Ah, but although I wanted ordinary, I still wanted you all to myself, so renting the alley was a compromise."

She muttered to herself as she finished lacing the first shoe.

"Do they fit?" he asked. "I called Parker for a size."

"Parker helped you out?"

"Yes. Now that we're not engaged—"

She interrupted him. "You were never engaged."

He ignored her and continued, "—we can be friends. Parker makes a good friend, I suspect."

"Not so good for me if she's supplying you with information."

"Would it make you feel better to know that she threatened me bodily harm if I hurt you?" he asked.

Shey smiled. "Yes, surprisingly enough, it would."

Tanner laughed. "Thought that might appeal."

She leaned over and finished tying her other shoe. A small strip of skin lay exposed between the bottom of her shirt and the top of her jeans. Very small and exposed by accident. It only made it more sexy.

Everything about Shey Carlson turned him on. Her bluster, her leather jacket, her laughter, her quick wit…and that small swatch of skin he couldn't seem to tear his gaze away from.

"No tattoo there," he said, more to himself than to her.

She turned and pulled her shirt down with a sharp snap. "I told you that you wouldn't find it unless I showed you, so stop looking."

"I like to look," he assured her.

She rolled her eyes and shook her head. "So are we going to bowl, or sit here and trade barbs all night?"

"Bowl," he announced. Maybe when she rolled the ball down the lane her shirt would pull up again.

"I might need a few lessons," he added.

"You've never bowled before?" Shey asked.

"Never."

"They don't bowl in Europe?"

"Yes, of course there's bowling. There's ten pin and even lawn bowling. I just haven't tried either."

"Probably too busy playing the princely sport of polo, or something."

There was no way he was going to admit he loved polo after that barb, so he simply ignored her goading.

She sighed a hefty put-upon sort of sigh. "Guess it's up to me to teach you about good old American bowling."

Two games later, Tanner managed his first strike. Oh, he didn't fool himself, it was pure luck, not skill, but it was enough to make him whoop with the success.

Shey just laughed. "You're still not going to break one hundred."

"A few more games and I'll be ready for the pro circuit," he assured her.

She laughed again and took her turn.

He'd been right. Bowling was a perfect first date.

And sitting on the bench, watching Shey roll her ball down the lane, he had to admit he'd never expected such a fine view in a bowling alley.

As if she could read his mind, she turned and said, "Stop looking at me."

"As you pointed out, I rented the whole alley. There's no one else to look at."

She shook her head as she took her seat. "Your turn."

Tanner got up and retrieved his ball. She was right, he might not break one hundred in the game, despite his first strike, but he thought he was scoring pretty darn high on the date. Her scowls didn't carry much heat. No, the biggest amount of heat was generated by his reaction to her nearness.

Living on the wild side, he reached out and ran a finger lightly down her cheek.

She pulled back. "Why'd you do that?"

"Because I've wanted to touch you all night, but I've been trying to be a gentleman."

She didn't say anything, and feeling emboldened, he set the ball back down, took her hand and pulled her out of the seat. "Know what else I've been dying to do?" he asked.

She didn't verbally respond, just shrugged.

"This."

He knew he probably shouldn't, that Shey wasn't ready to admit there was something between them.

But he couldn't stop himself. He'd pulled her into his arms and claimed her lips before he could have second thoughts.

This was no introduction. They'd moved far beyond that.

It was a kiss driven by need, by a hunger that seemed to grow the more he was with her.

Shey knew kissing a prince was foolhardy—she'd known it every time she kissed him. But the moment her lips touched his—she forgot. She just didn't care.

She couldn't even begin to think about all the reasons why she shouldn't be in his arms. All she could think about was this man, this moment…this kiss.

She could feel his desire and rather than make her want to back away it simply fueled her own longings. She wanted Tanner more than she'd ever wanted anyone, anything.

Standing, wrapped in his arms…it felt like coming home. As if this was what had been missing all her life. This man, this moment.

Standing in a deserted bowling alley, wearing her new bowling shoes, kissing a prince.

She couldn't imagine anything more that she could ever want.

She twined her arms around his neck and pulled

him even tighter. She wanted to meld her body to his, to get so close that she couldn't tell where her body ended and his began.

He made a small noise in the back of his throat. A groan that didn't speak of pain but of passion. It heated her blood even more.

He pulled back a moment, and whispered her name.

That's all he said, but there was so much wrapped up in that one word. In her name.

She loosened one hand and stroked his cheek. Her fingers were abraded by the faintest hint of stubble. "I think we'd best finish the game before we both go further than we want to go."

"I can't think of any distance I wouldn't be willing to go for you."

She didn't know how to answer that, so she didn't even try. She sat back on the bench and nodded her head toward his bowling ball. "Your turn."

For a moment, she thought he was going to protest, to push her. She had to admit it wouldn't take much pushing to have her back in his arms. But he didn't. He simply picked up his ball. She felt a secret sort of satisfaction that she had him so rattled his ball went directly into the gutter.

His superiority was short-lived when she did the same.

"I think dinner's here," he said.

Two men wheeled in a cart with silver domes covering large plates.

"I don't think this is normal bowling procedure."

"I might have wanted an ordinary first date, but there's only so much ordinary I can take."

Dinner was a five-star affair. Dishes appeared that Shey had never heard of and certainly had never tasted. Salmon covered with a delicate sauce. Some ricey sort of dish with all sorts of stuff in it. A light, white wine.

It definitely wasn't burgers and soda. But maybe, she admitted to herself, it was a nice change.

They ate in silence for a while.

Shey kept sneaking glances at Tanner. He looked so tempting. She had this outrageous urge to lean across the table and kiss him again. To kiss him and more.

She'd like—

"Can I ask you a question without ruining the night?" Tanner asked, interrupting her fantasies.

"I can't guarantee anything in the way of answers," Shey said, "but go ahead and shoot."

"Why?" Tanner asked.

She was about to ask "Why what?" when he said, "Why are you so secretive about all you do for the community?"

Again he anticipated her question and added, "The people at the back of the store, for instance."

"I'm not doing it for the community. They're just folks who need a hand. I'm simply in a position to give it to them."

"Not everyone would even notice their need."

"Do you know what it's like to go hungry?" she asked softly. "I do. After my dad died, there were times when there wasn't much in the house, especially the day before payday. My mom would try and save whatever there was for me, but I caught on. I made sure I had 'study dates' those nights and would tell her I'd eaten at a friend's house. I'd itemize the entire dinner, describe the way it tasted and smelled so she'd be convinced I'd eaten."

"But there's so much here, in this country," he said.

"And we have an entire class of working poor—people whose paychecks don't quite make it through a whole week. We have people who are hungry, just like everywhere else."

"And when you meet them, you feed them?" It came out as a question, but it was more of a statement.

Shey shrugged and tried to look nonchalant. She didn't like it that he knew this about her, but she liked it even less that he was making so much of it. "It's nothing. A few sandwiches. It's just the kind of thing most people do."

"Not all people." He paused. "How about the literacy?"

"I—" she said, ready to blow him off. But there was this intensity about him as he watched her, waiting for an answer. And she knew he'd simply deflect any attempt she might make to hide behind her wit. She bowed to the inevitable without even trying not to answer.

"There was a girl in my class, she was always behind, never quite up to speed. She and I, we were both outsiders, and eventually we came together. We sort of hung out."

"You, an outsider?" he asked.

"Hand-me-down clothes and a chip on my shoulder. Plus I was smart and wouldn't pretend otherwise. Smart and a smart-ass. I didn't really endear myself to anyone." She could laugh about it now, but back then it hurt.

"Your friend?" he prompted.

"One day I watched her mouthing the words that she was reading and realized she had problems. Like Lawrence, she could read enough to get by—barely. But she missed the joy of reading. It was a chore. We worked together and eventually she found the beauty in books."

"You're amazing." There was a look in his eyes that made her uncomfortable.

Shey felt embarrassed. "Oh, don't go all princy on me and start showering me with false praise. And I wasn't amazing, just lucky. I had an amazing mom who loved me."

"More lucky than you know," Tanner said.

There was something in his voice that prompted her to say, "Tell me about your parents."

"They're—" He shrugged. "They're busy. My father's been instrumental in restructuring our government. Dragging it kicking and screaming into the new millennium. My mother's always here or there."

"And where do you fit in?" she asked.

"I'm the heir. I have duties and obligations. That's what my family is about, duty and obligation."

"What about love?" she asked softly.

"Yes," he said slowly. "I suppose. We're just not very demonstrative with it. We have a formal relationship."

"You sound as if you wished it were different."

"That's why I accepted the idea of me and Parker. I'd seen her family and I knew that's what I wanted for my children, what she grew up with. The kind of thing you grew up with."

"Parker and I couldn't have had more different childhoods," Shey assured him.

"But you both had parents who were fierce in their love."

She reached out and held his hand, a gentle touch, and they sat in silence for a while. Two people content to just be together.

Shey started, "You know, all my mother ever wanted was to have my dad back. I think she missed him until the day she died. I wanted to give her the world, to make her life easier, to show her so many things. I never got the chance."

"Don't you know that you already did that and more? She saw the whole thing, the beauty, the hope, the possibilities every time she looked at you. She saw your father in you, as well. But more important, she saw love…it's what I see when I look at you. The beauty, the hope, the possibilities and the—"

Shey was suddenly nervous again. She didn't want to hear what else he saw. So she interrupted. "Maybe you need glasses. You seem to be seeing an awful lot of funny things."

"Don't be afraid to let me in," he tried.

"I'm not afraid of anything," Shey said.

"Prove it," Tanner challenged. "Kiss me."

"Kissing you will prove what?" she asked, trying to sound as if kissing him was the last thing she'd ever want to do; all the while, it was *all* she wanted to do.

"That you're not afraid of me."

"Afraid? Ha."

"So what are you waiting for?"

An attack of good sense would be the logical answer, but all her sense, good and bad, had seemingly fled. Shey found herself moving back into Tanner's arms.

It felt like coming home.

* * *

"Tonight changes things—you know that, don't you?" Tanner asked as Shey got out of the car an hour later.

"It doesn't have to," she said, wanting to believe it. Needing to believe it. "We're just two people who've discovered they have chemistry."

"It's more than that. There's something bigger between us. It's been there since the first time I climbed on the back of your motorbike. And being with you has only made it grow bigger."

"I've got to go in now."

"Are you going to invite me in? Maybe you'd best go back to keeping an eye on me. An eye and any other body parts you'd like to share."

"You're exhausting, you know that?"

"Just trying to wear you down with my winning ways."

"Good night, Tanner."

"Spoilsport."

"I had a good time." She was surprised to hear herself say the words. But they were the truth. She'd enjoyed herself thoroughly. Being with Tanner. She could get used to it.

But she'd better not. He was leaving soon. "I've got to go."

"I might not have done a lot of dating in America,

but it seems to me there's a certain protocol that should be observed."

"Protocol?"

"A good-night kiss."

"I think there's been enough kissing for one night. More than enough."

"Fine," he said and shot her a tragic look. "My first ordinary—"

She scoffed, but he continued, "—ordinary date and you're going to ignore custom."

"Fine," she said, trying to sound disgruntled even though she didn't think she'd quite carried it off. A smile kept twitching on her lips.

She gave him a quick peck on the cheek.

He just shook his head and tsked. "That's the best you can do?"

This time the smile didn't just twitch, it erupted and Shey gave into temptation and kissed him as though she meant it. "Now, that's a good-night kiss for the record books," she said, pleased with the slightly dazed expression the prince now wore.

"Definitely for the record books," he murmured. "And I'll look forward to that other American custom."

"What's that?" she asked, knowing she shouldn't.

"A kiss hello tomorrow."

"About tomorrow. I think I need the day off."

"Perfect. We'll go—"

"The day off from you. I need time to think. There seems to be a definite lack of thinking when I'm with you."

She expected him to protest, to fight.

Instead he just said, "Fine. But I'll be back on Monday and we're going to settle a few things. While you're thinking, ask yourself what it is that's scaring you so badly."

"I'm not—"

He interrupted her protest and simply said, "Good night, Shey."

No more talk about kissing. No protests about spending a day apart. Just good-night.

Shey unlocked her door and stomped into the house. The house that suddenly felt empty.

Empty. That's just how she wanted it.

No more annoying princes tailing her every move, filling her quiet house with a lot of noise.

She tossed her jacket on the hook and sat on the couch without even bothering to turn a light on.

Think about what was scaring her?

Ha.

She wasn't afraid of anything.

And at the top of her list of things she wasn't afraid of were fiancée-seeking-princes who had no idea of what comprised an ordinary date. There wasn't an ordinary bone in His Royal Painness's body.

As a matter of fact, he was quite extraordinary.

Even as she thought it, she realized that it had nothing to do with his royalty, and everything to do with the man himself.

If he were anyone else, Shey might allow herself to have feelings for him.

No, if he were anyone else, he wouldn't be Tanner and she wouldn't care a bit.

Okay, so if he wasn't a prince.

No, that wasn't right, either. Being a prince was part of who he was. Just like having dark brown eyes—chestnut eyes—was part of him. His sense of humor. The way he touched her, as if she were something beautiful and precious.

All the little pieces that in and of themselves might not be exceptional, came together to make a man she could—

The phone rang.

Saved by the bell.

She couldn't afford admission of—well, anything regarding Tanner.

"Hello?" she asked. Hoping it was Parker or Cara. They could be counted on to talk a long time and distract her from her thoughts.

"Is Tanner there?" a male voice asked.

It didn't sound like one of his guards. After an

evening of poker with them, she thought she'd recognize Emil, Peter or Tonio.

"Who's calling, please?" she asked. She wasn't
going to give information about Tanner out to just
anyone.

"His father. He's not answering his mobile and his
men said that I should try this number. That he's been
spending a lot of time here."

"I wouldn't say a lot. And he's not here now. You
can probably catch him in a few minutes at the
hotel."

She thought Tanner's father would say all right
and hang up. Instead he said, "Do you mind if I ask
who you are and what you are to my son?"

"I'm Shey Carlson. A friend of Parker's. And I guess
you could say I'm a friend of your son's, as well."

"So you're helping match them up?"

"No, I wouldn't say that."

"What would you say?"

"I'd say the idea of arranging a marriage is ar-
chaic. That both Parker and Tanner deserve more than
an appropriate union. They deserve love."

"Love needs some common ground, a foundation.
That's what Parker's parents and I were hoping they'd
find. A common background, something to build a relationship on." He paused a moment and added, "I
want my son to be happy."

"I do, too. I just don't think it's going to happen between him and Parker."

"But his men said he went out on a romantic date."

"I don't know about romantic," she said, thinking about bowling shoes. "And I wouldn't put much stock in the date. But I'm afraid your son's coming home soon without a fiancée. And even though you didn't ask, let me say he deserves love. Both in a marriage and from his parents."

"I love my son."

"Maybe it's time you mentioned that to him," she said softly. "Goodbye, Your Highness."

And she hung up.

Hung up on a king. And shouldn't she have called him Your Majesty? She should probably learn more royal protocol. Not that it mattered.

Next on her list was breaking up with a prince. Sure, they weren't really together, but she had to make it clear that they couldn't see each other anymore. Because there was no way his father, much less his kingdom, would want someone like Shey as their princess.

Knowing what she had to do didn't mean she wanted to do it, because Shey was beginning to suspect that breaking things off with Tanner would break her heart.

Chapter Eight

"Men…" Parker growled the next afternoon.

They closed the shops early on Sundays and the three of them had gathered around a cluster of couches in Cara's bookstore.

This was what Shey needed…to reconnect with her friends. She was sure they'd help her regain her sanity and was heartened when Parker started the conversation with the proper amount of frustration fused into just that one word.

"Men," Parker said again.

"Yeah, men," Shey agreed.

Actually, man. Tanner.

She must have been off her rocker to think she

could just date a prince…especially this prince. He'd come to Erie looking for a fiancée, a significant other. And now that Parker was out of the running he thought Shey would step up?

She didn't know much, but she was absolutely sure she wasn't a second-string kind of girlfriend, any more than she was a dating-a-prince sort of girl.

"Men…" Cara sighed, all breathy and dreamy.

Shey glared at her. That was not the proper tone for the conversation.

Derision. Annoyance. But she wasn't in the mood for romantic notions. Today, she didn't want to hear anything nice about the male species.

Cara didn't seem intimidated by Shey's best glare. "Hey, just because you two have men problems, doen't mean I do. I'm still looking for my Mr. Right."

"So am I," Shey assured her.

Because there was no way His Royal Kiss Me-Ness was it. She wanted a man who liked Harleys.

Although Tanner did seem to enjoy her bike.

Okay, so she wanted a man who enjoyed the simple pleasures.

Remembering Tanner's enthusiasm on the boat, at the concert and even bowling—it made her feel decidedly uncomfortable, because Tanner certainly wasn't the man she wanted.

"Me, too," Parker said.

"Come on," Cara said with a lot more force than Cara generally used. "You two may be having problems, but believe me, you're definitely off the market. Love's not always easy."

"Love?" Parker asked, her voice much higher than normal.

"Yes, love," Cara assured her. "You and Shey've got it bad."

"Ha," Parker said.

Shey couldn't agree more. "Yeah, ha."

In love with Tanner?

She'd be a fool.

Cara continued on her must-be-love speech even after Shelly joined them. Shey was pretty sure she kept up her end of the conversation, but she couldn't be sure. Her brain was sort of trying to wrap itself around her feelings for Tanner.

He frustrated the hell out of her.

He made her laugh.

He was annoyingly persistent.

Gorgeous as all get-out.

She'd been surprised to discover she liked him. But something more than that?

She wasn't that foolish.

Loving a prince would be absurd.

She just wasn't going to do it. The warm melty

feeling she got whenever he kissed her, whenever she was with him, well, she'd simply ignore it.

Shey Carlson was not going to fall in love with a prince.

Shey couldn't stand any more love-talk and made her escape. For the first time ever, talking to her friends hadn't comforted her.

As a matter of fact, Cara's whole love-and-you're-off-the-market speech had left her feeling more uneasy than ever.

She wasn't quite sure what to do with herself.

She didn't want to go home.

Didn't want to go back into the shops.

She wanted to find Tanner, to be with him. Instead, she practically bumped into Peter.

"Did Tanner send you to spy on me?" she asked. Not sure whether she preferred a yes or no answer.

"No."

Her heart did a little dip. She must have been hoping for the yes, which didn't make sense. She'd told Tanner to give her a day off and he had.

She should be pleased.

The fact that she wasn't didn't make sense.

But then nothing about her feelings for Tanner made sense.

"Okay." She started walking back down the path through the park again.

"Hey," Peter said, causing her to stop and turn back around. "Is Shelly still in there?"

"Yes."

He grinned. "Well, then, okay."

"Why don't you just go in and get her?"

"She told me to give her some space." He sounded as morose as Shey felt.

"And you think stalking her qualifies?" she asked.

"I was waiting for her to get off work, hoping she'd had enough space already."

She thought of Cara's little speech and decided maybe her friend hadn't been entirely wrong. There was something brewing between Peter and Shelly.

"Man, you've got it bad," she murmured.

"Sort of the pot calling the cat black, isn't it?"

"Kettle," Shey replied, even though she knew what he meant.

"What?" Peter asked.

"The saying is, the pot calling the kettle black."

"Oh." He shrugged. "Either way, I've been watching you and Tanner, and I think I'm not the only one developing feelings."

"But that's the point. Nothing could ever develop between Tanner and me."

"I don't know if we have a lot of say in matters of the heart." He sounded remarkably like romance-on-the-brain Cara.

"I gotta go," Shey said. She started down the path again without a backward glance.

Love on the brains.

Everyone she met seemed to have it. Even Parker seemed all sighy over her private investigator.

Well, enough was enough.

Shey refused to get all mush-for-brains over Tanner. She was going to ignore whatever it was she was feeling and simply wait for him to leave. Encourage him to leave, even.

After all, he'd have to leave soon.

Wouldn't he?

Tanner sat on a bench at the tip of the dock. A giant statue of a dolphin sat to his right. He wondered why the city chose something that didn't live in a fresh-water lake for a statue.

It was an inane thing to think about, but it was easier to ponder dolphins than to wonder about Shey Carlson.

She was an enigma. Every time he thought he'd figured her out, she presented a new piece of the puzzle…a piece he hadn't even realized was missing until he found it.

Yesterday's date had been the right way to approach her. Traditional wooing would never work with Shey. But bowling…it was brilliant, if he did say so himself.

Now he had to think of something equally as original for tomorrow night. He needed something special because he had to talk to her about how he felt.

When he'd met her, he'd found Shey frustrating but entertaining. It didn't take long for the entertaining to grow, and a healthy dose of respect to move in. Oh, she still frustrated him, but on a totally man-falling-for-a-woman level.

He wasn't falling any longer. And he knew the exact minute he'd stopped.

When she'd made those sandwiches for the men. He'd stopped falling and hit the hard realization that he loved her.

He'd come to Erie to woo Parker, a princess, someone who would be the perfect wife for him.

Instead he'd found Shey. Brash, bold and independent. And he'd fallen. But she was stubborn. And convincing her that they belonged together might take some work.

Okay, no might about it. Loving Shey was easy. Convincing her that they belonged together would be a bit harder.

He needed to find something perfect, some perfect date where he could lay out his case.

Looking out along the bay's shoreline, he could just make out the tip of the amphitheater's tent.

And he remembered what Shey had said. He flipped out his cell phone. "Tonio, I need you to make a few calls for me…"

Shey tried to walk off some of her nervous energy. She loved her downtown neighborhood. It was a brisk walk over to the bay. Watching the water never failed to soothe her, and she really needed soothing today.

She walked down State Street, past the hospital and down the hill. The Bicentennial Tower stood, tall and proud at the foot of the dock. Cars filled the spaces, people milled about, some fishing, some walking, and several sitting at the outdoor tables of the restaurants.

Nope. She didn't feel soothed. Nothing today was normal. If anything, she felt as if her restlessness had escalated. She felt itchy with it.

Yep, Tanner had made her itchy, like some dread disease. He'd infected her.

She'd see him tomorrow and make sure he understood that yesterday was an aberration. There would be no more dating, no more kissing. It was time for him to head home and get back to the business of being a prince. And it was time for her to…

Miss him.

She could try and talk herself out of it, try to convince herself it wasn't so, but the truth was, she'd miss him a lot. She'd miss his laughter, his company. She'd miss trading barbs. She missed trading kisses with him even now.

She walked along the edge of the dock and wondered how it had happened.

How did Shey Carlson fall for a prince?

It was ridiculous.

She was going to stop right now.

A bunch of gulls cried out as they swooped down onto the sidewalk and gobbled up some spilt popcorn. Their cries seemed to mock her, laugh at her. She might try, but she couldn't stop the feelings she had for Tanner.

It might be ridiculous, might have happened way too fast, but what she felt was real. And it was growing.

Part of her wished he was here with her right now, and part of her wished she wouldn't have to face him again, because when she did she was going to have to send him away.

"Shey?"

As if some genie had been listening there he was. Tanner was at her side, smiling. "I was just thinking about you," he said.

She was about to admit she'd been thinking about him as well, so she didn't say anything.

"Can you get tomorrow night off from the store? Get Shelly or that college student to handle the evening hours?"

"Why?"

"Because I have plans for us."

"About that—" Now…she'd tell him now. His comment made for the perfect segue…she'd tell him there was no *us*. The only plans he needed to make were plans to go home.

But he stood there, watching her, waiting, and she couldn't make herself tell him to go. Tomorrow. She'd let herself have one more night with him, then she'd tell him to go home.

"About that?" he prompted.

"I'm sure I can get someone to cover things. So are you going to tell me what we'll be doing?"

"No. But if you stop looking so nervous and smile at me, I'll buy you an ice cream."

Despite the fact she knew she shouldn't, she smiled, her heart feeling lighter than it had all day. "You've got yourself a deal."

He offered her his hand. "Shall we?"

She took it and felt the now familiar zing of awareness as she touched him.

She'd finally found a man she could love and for both their sakes she was going to have to send him away.

But not until tomorrow. Tonight, she was going to simply enjoy his company and the ice cream.

"Let's go."

Chapter Nine

"Is everything ready?" Tanner asked Emil. They were at Monarch's and he was nervously waiting for Shey to get ready.

For years he'd thought he was pretty good with women. He didn't lose his cool. He knew how to woo them. But with Shey, he hadn't just lost it, his cool had totally been obliterated with no hope of retrieval. And he didn't have a clue how to woo her. He was just shooting in the dark.

"Everything just as you wanted it," Emil said, a soothing, I'm-talking-to-a-madman quality to his tone. "The driver's waiting out front."

Tanner didn't care that his friends were starting

to worry about his sanity, all he cared about was Shey, convincing her that they had something rare together.

"Good," he said. "Now comes the hard part."

"Hard part?" Emil asked.

"Convincing the lady to come along." And knowing Shey, *hard part* was an understatement. Her stubbornness was one of the qualities he loved about her—except when he didn't. And he suspected tonight was going to be one of the *didn't* nights.

"What woman wouldn't want an evening like tonight?" Emil asked.

Tanner laughed. "Shey Carlson. I expect she's going to come along kicking and screaming the whole time."

"So why would you plan a night like this for a woman who's not going to enjoy it?"

"I suspect she'll enjoy it, but I know she won't admit it. The thing is every woman, whether they admit to wanting it or not, deserves a piece of magic now and again." At least he hoped every woman—specifically Shey—wanted magic.

Emil was still shaking his head. "Good luck, then. Sounds like you're going to need it." He turned and walked toward the door of the shop.

"I am," Tanner muttered more to himself than to Emil. "I guarantee I am."

"You are what?" Shey asked as she came back into the room.

"Are you done here?" he asked, ignoring her question.

"Yes. And I know I said I'd go out with you tonight, but I've been thinking about it and I don't think it's a good idea. We—"

He cut her off by planting a big kiss on her lips. He meant it to be a playful way of silencing her, but the moment his lips met hers, all thoughts of playfulness evaporated and all that he could focus on was the woman in front of him, the woman he wrapped his arms around and pulled closer.

He let himself sink into her, lose himself in her.

This woman, his entire body—his entire being— seemed to cry out. *This woman.* He couldn't get enough of her, couldn't pull her close enough.

She seemed to feel it, too. Her arms were around his neck, her body pressed willingly to his. She moaned a little as he deepened the kiss.

Gradually he eased back, fingers twisted in her short hair. He smiled. "I'm asking, Shey. Please come with me. There's so much we need to talk about. And I think you'll agree that this…whatever this is between us should be discussed."

"Where do you want to go?" she asked, not exactly agreeing.

"Trust me."

* * *

Trust me?

Why on earth had she said yes and come with the crazy prince? Because she was crazier than he was.

Trust me?

She was riding through Erie in the back of a limo wearing a blindfold. How on earth had she let herself get talked into this situation?

"Tanner, this is silly."

"Leave it on, Shey."

"You can't make me," she said, trying to sound put out, when all the time she felt like smiling.

Maybe even laughing.

He was so obviously pleased with whatever he'd planned. "I could take it off if I wanted. You're not making me keep it on."

"According to you I'm an arrogant prince who thinks he can do anything…so, yes, I guess I do think I can make you."

"Maybe I thought that once, the part about you being an arrogant prince, not the part about your being able to make me. But I don't think that anymore." This whole blindfold thing had some perks. She couldn't see his expression as she said the words—mushy words that weren't like her at all.

"You don't think I'm arrogant?" he asked.

She didn't need to see him to hear his smile. She could feel it and it warmed her. "No, not anymore."

She paused half a beat and added, "But before you climb on some sort of pedestal, I still think you're a pain and more than a bit the spoiled, pampered prince." Ah, that was better.

"But not arrogant. That must mean I'm growing on you."

The man was impossible to insult. Shey didn't know why she bothered trying, but even though she doubted it would work, she tried one last parting shot. "Yes, you've grown on me—rather like a fungus, yes."

"Ah, Shey, you do have a way with words. I worry that all your compliments will go to my head."

"You're trying to sidetrack me and it's not working. Where are you taking me?"

"You're not very good at surprises," he said.

"I never had a lot of chances to learn," she said.

"Maybe I want to make it up to you? Maybe I want to give you more than just a few surprises…maybe I want to give you the whole world."

Shey snorted and forced herself to say, "Did you memorize that line from some book? If so, I'd get my money back. It didn't work."

And that was a big fat lie. He'd pretty much racked her insides with that line. But Shey wasn't about to let him know that. He knew too much already.

"I don't need my money back. Seeing you smile like that was worth every penny."

"I wasn't smiling." At least she didn't think she'd smiled. After all, being blindfolded didn't mean you lost your ability to sense your own facial expressions...did it?

Oh, her Prince Charming wannabe was addling her brains. She had to be careful. Very careful. She sensed that whatever he was planning was designed to turn her into a woman who would succumb to his scheme.

"Here we go," he said.

She realized the car had come to a stop. He helped her out.

"Can I take off the blindfold now?"

"Not quite yet."

She wasn't sure why she complied, but she let him lead her forward. They were inside now, Shey realized. "Now?"

He pulled off the blindfold. "I thought we'd have a picnic."

She took in her surroundings. An ornate lobby with mirrors and a huge, winding staircase. She knew exactly where they were.

"You think we're going to picnic in the Warner?"

The Warner Theater was a lady of a certain age who'd recently had a major face-lift. Shey had season tickets to the Philharmonic and had loved watching the process of the theater's revitalization.

"You know, the first time I came to the Warner was with a school field trip. We saw *Giselle*. I remember how my breath just sort of sucked out of me with a whoosh. I fell in love with ballet, with classical music that day."

"I know all about falling," he said, a strange husky catch in his voice.

"Tanner," Shey started to say, but then wasn't sure, so she stopped.

"Come on," he invited, leading her toward the stairs. "Let's have dinner. We have to talk."

"You know I've never found anything good followed the phrase, 'we have to talk.'"

He was going to tell her he was leaving.

Well, that was good. He was a prince and he had a job to do. A country that was counting on him. Yes, it was better that he left now, because each day he stayed would only make their parting harder.

Okay, so tonight was their farewell date. Maybe there'd be a farewell kiss, too. Then that would be it. Tanner would go back to Amar and Parker would stay here in Erie where she belonged.

Mission accomplished.

Shey should be ecstatic.

For some odd reason, she wasn't.

"Maybe the news won't be as bad as you think," he said, all cryptic.

"I sort of doubt it." Oh, yeah, he was leaving all right. And of course he'd think she'd think that was good news.

And she should.

But she didn't.

As he led her to a blanket he'd spread at the back of the balcony she realized they actually were having a picnic. The big picnic hamper made it a pretty easy guess.

Shey noticed there were people on the stage.

"What's up with them?"

"Your Philharmonic is having a dress rehearsal. I thought you might enjoy some music with our dinner."

As if on cue, the orchestra struck up a song.

"Nice," she said.

Tanner poured two glasses of wine and handed one to Shey.

"To a magical night," he toasted.

Shey reluctantly clinked glasses with him. "Tanner, we've been over this, you're leaving for home soon. There can't be too much magic."

"Whenever I'm with you, there's magic."

"Oh, come on. Was that from the same book? Geesh, you definitely need to take it back to the bookstore. That was just lame."

He chuckled. "Okay, flowery prose isn't going to

impress you. Tell me, Shey, what else can I do to make an impression on you?"

"Why would you want to make an impression on me? I just don't get it."

"Don't you?" he asked, taking a sip of the wine and sighing his pleasure. "You're an amazing woman."

"And you're a prince who's looking for a wife. I'm not her, so what is this?"

"Two people enjoying each other's company." He took another sip. "Drink your wine."

She did. It was as perfect as she'd expected. The rest of the meal was, as well. This was no cold-food picnic. The food was hot and five-star. No salmon this time, instead it was some beef dish, with potatoes and vegetables that were crisp and fresh. And dessert was a chocolate cake that would make any woman weep with the utter decadence of it.

They ate in companionable silence, enjoying the meal and the music.

"I don't think I can have another bite," Shey said. Despite herself, and her better sense, she'd enjoyed the food, the atmosphere and—she hated to admit it—the company.

"I'd like to pick up an earlier subject."

"Which subject? Space exploration? I'm all for it.

People need new horizons to explore. It's the last frontier."

"Not space…us."

"Tanner, this has been a special night, let's not ruin it by talking about things that will never happen. You're leaving and I'd like to think we've become friends."

"You're right, I am leaving."

Yeah, she'd known she was right. This was just his kiss-'em-then-leave-'em dinner.

"I figured. I mean, you've accepted you and Parker won't work and you have duties in your country. I know I sniped at you, but I enjoyed that you sniped right back. I had a lot of fun." She stood. "And dinner was a nice touch. But if you don't mind, I'd like to go home now. I have to open the store tomorrow."

"Shey—" he started.

"Nope, don't say another word. Especially from whatever book you've been quoting from all night. Just a quick goodbye will do it."

He stood as well. Stood an inch away from her. There was a challenge in his eye. And though Shey would have liked to back away, to distance herself from Tanner, she couldn't.

"I am leaving, but not alone. I'd like to take you with me." He reached into his pocket and withdrew a ring.

"Shey—"

"Don't say it…not one word. I can't believe you'd give me a ring you meant for Parker. As if you promised to go home with a fiancée and any woman would do."

"I went out and bought this for you, and I assure you just any woman wouldn't do."

"Oh. Well, still, put it away."

"I've learned a thing or two about you, Shey Carlson. You want the world to think you're tough, but that hard shell is just protection because in reality, you're all heart."

She could feel her cheeks heat up. Blushing like some schoolgirl. This man was messing with her mind.

"You don't know what you're taking about," she tried to growl, but it came out less than growly. As a matter of fact, it sounded sort of soft and tearful.

"Sure I do," he said, all cocky and confident. "I've seen you with the people you help out with, with the people you work with, with your friends… You're all heart, Shey. That's what I see when you're with them. You care. You cared enough to keep me from trying to talk Parker into something that would have made her miserable. You're right, she's not ready for royal life."

She glanced at the ring, then back at him. "Well, neither am I."

"You're wrong. You have so much to offer. Remember what you said about Parker walking away from the chance to give her causes a forum? You could do that. Could give so much. Most importantly, you could give your heart. Not just to my country, but to me. I want your heart, Shey."

"Tanner, I can't." From mushy she was moving right on to weepy. Now, genuine tears filled her eyes. She could feel them, but she'd be darned if she'd let them fall.

"Answer me this," he said. "Even though it's happened fast, do you love me?"

She shrugged. "I won't answer, because it doesn't matter."

"How can you say that?" he asked, running a hand along her cheek. "Love always matters, Shey."

"Your people deserve a princess. Someone to represent them to the world. I can't imagine that would be me."

"I can imagine enough for both of us. Think about it, instead of feeding a few folks at your back door, you'd be able to promote programs that would feed a multitude. Rather than teaching one man to read, you can lend your support to programs that will teach many. Think about all you could do."

"I don't do those things for recognition, but because I know what it's like to be down on your luck, to need a hand up."

"I know that, but you'll have a larger stage to offer those hand-ups. And you'd have me." He paused a moment and added, "Maybe that's the problem. Having me. Loving me."

"That's not the problem. Your saying that I should marry you because it will give me a forum to promote my causes to a larger audience, that's the problem. Your thinking I should marry you because of all the good I could do if I were your wife and a princess."

"That's just a bonus. I'm saying you should marry me because I love you and can't imagine a life without you. And if you're honest with yourself, I think you'd have to admit you love me, as well."

"You know I want you. I think I've more than proven that." She couldn't avoid admitting that, even if she couldn't confess everything to him.

"Then say yes," he said.

"I—"

"Shey, I tried to leave, but couldn't."

"You swore you'd go home with a fiancée, and you're just trying to make good on that vow."

"It's not some promise to my father. It's you. I want you with me. You're right, I came looking for a fiancée. I came here looking for you. I just didn't know it."

"I can't be a princess," she admitted.

"Fine," he said with a shrug. "Then I'll quit."

"You can't do that," Shey said.

"Sure I can. Parker did."

"We've talked about this, her brother's next in line, not her. It's not the same. You're it. Your father's only child."

"So? I have cousins that can stand in as heirs." He took her hand. "Don't you see, you're what matters."

"You can't give it up."

"I wouldn't be the first prince to do it."

"But—"

"Don't you get it?" he asked, his voice filled with emotion. "I'd give up anything for you. Do anything to win you. Say yes, you'll marry me and I'll stay here and work at Monarch's. I'll be your busboy, and you can make sandwiches. We'd be happy. I swear it."

She laughed, then looked in his eyes and realized just how serious he was. "You'd do that. You'd really do that?"

"To be with you? Yes. I'd do that and more."

"Yes," she whispered, knowing she couldn't fight against the feelings that were practically exploding in her chest. "Yes," she said louder.

"Yes," he repeated. "I'd do that and more. Tell me what it will take and—"

"I guess it will take princess-lessons for me. I'm sure Parker will give me a start if I ask, but I'll need someone to help me with the advanced lessons when we get home to Amar. I don't want to embarrass you or your family. And speaking of your family, have you given any thought to what they're going to say when you come home with me, rather than Parker?"

"After you had that little talk with my father, I don't imagine they'll risk incurring your wrath again."

"Oh. I'd forgotten about that." She knew she shouldn't have talked that way to a king, to Tanner's father. "He'll never forget that."

"No, I'm sure he won't." He paused as her words hit him. "Wait a minute. When you said yes, were you saying yes you'll marry me? I mean it wasn't just some elaborate plan to get rid of me?"

"Yes, I'll marry you. It's too soon and I think you're probably going to live to regret it, but I can't imagine not having you around."

"Yes," he said, and ran to the edge of the balcony. "She said yes," he called down.

The orchestra stopped in midsong and started a new one. A very classical-sounding version of "Margaritaville."

Shey started laughing. "What are you doing?"

"I arranged to have them play our song."

"We have a song?" she asked. She looked at Tanner and knew that despite the fact that she had misgivings about marrying a prince, she didn't have one single doubt about marrying the man…this man.

"Sure we have a song," he said, pulling her into his arms. "Unless there's another Jimmy Buffet tune you'd like to choose?"

She laughed. "No, this one's fine. Our song."

"They can play it at the wedding."

Oh, gosh she'd agreed to marry him, but hadn't thought beyond that. A wedding. "What on earth will people think?"

"I don't know and I don't care."

He held out the ring. "Say the words," he commanded.

She obliged him, knowing the poor guy was going to suffer a lot from her not being so obliging in the future. Tonight, she couldn't argue with him about anything. Her heart was just too full. "Yes, I'll marry you."

"No, the other ones. Say the words."

She realized that she hadn't vocalized what she'd felt since…well, probably since the moment she met him. "I love you."

"Again."

"Geesh, you're bossy. Someone might think you were a prince or something. But for the record, I love you. It's kind of crazy, but I love you and will marry you."

"And if you're worrying about regrets, just ask me in fifty years if I have any and I'm pretty sure the only one I'll have is not finding you sooner." He slipped the ring on her finger.

"There goes that darned book again. Just how many cheesy quotes are in it?" she asked, admiring the discreet diamond on her finger.

"I'm pretty sure the book has a lifetime's worth."

She sighed. "Well, then I guess I'll just have to get used to hearing you be cheesy every day."

"Every day," he promised. "I love you, Shey Carlson."

"And I love you, Tanner Ericson. I'd try for your whole title, but it's more than a mouthful."

"You'll have a lifetime to learn it. Princess Shey."

"Oh, my gosh. What did I sign up for?"

"My cheesy quote book would suggest I say, 'You signed up for a lifetime of love.'"

She groaned as she kissed her own bona fide Prince Charming, and, despite their differences, she knew their story would end with a very cheesy happily ever after.

Epilogue

Parker and Jace waved goodbye as Tanner and Shey both got on her motorcycle. She let him drive. Okay, driving was a generous description. She was teaching him, but he wasn't a fast learner.

They'd just put Cara on the plane for Eliason. She was going to help plan a small, private wedding for Parker and Jace, as well as for Tanner and Shey.

The four of them were hoping the small ruse would keep the paparazzi off their trail. Later there'd be some big ornate celebration, but for now, Shey just wanted to be surrounded by friends and family as she made her vows to Tanner.

"Hey," he said. "You promised to show me your

tattoo after we got Cara on the plane. As your fiancé I have a right to know. We can go back to my hotel, or to your place so you can show me in private."

"No privacy required," she assured him.

He'd spent the last few months speculating on what and where it was located. It was driving him nuts. And Shey might have admitted she loved him, but she also freely admitted that she loved teasing him.

"What do you mean, no privacy required?"

She pulled the collar of her shirt back from her neck toward her right shoulder. There, just above her shoulder blade, was a small crown. Tiny. Parker had insisted they all do something reckless when they'd opened up Monarch's and Titles, so the three of them had all gotten matching, pinky-nail-size crowns tattooed out of sight.

Tanner was smiling, the smile turned to a chuckle, then to laughter.

"You see, I came to Erie to find my princess and I did. You've even got the crown to prove it."

Shey laughed. "Just drive the bike, Prince Charming. And don't grind the gears this time."

"Your wish is my command…princess."

* * * * *

*Turn the page for a sneak peek
at Cara's story, available from
Silhouette Romance in September 2005!*

Prologue

Cara Phillips looked out the window of the plane as it made its approach to Eliason, a small European country that most of the world overlooked.

But to Cara, Eliason was magical.

A real-life kingdom.

For a minute she wondered what it would be like to have an entire land and know that it was yours… your responsibility, handed down generation after generation. Yours to protect, to guide, to cherish.

Cara's best friend, Parker Dillon, had been born here. Parker was a princess. Princess Marie Anna Parker Mickovich Dillonetti of Eliason.

But Parker had turned away from her legacy and chased after her dreams…dreams that had led her to

Perry Square in Erie, Pennsylvania, and to Jace O'Donnell, the man she was going to marry in just a month.

Four short weeks.

Their friend Shey Carlson and her fiancé, Tanner Ericson, were going to be married, as well.

A double ceremony.

Cara's romantic heart gave a small twist.

Truly, Parker and Shey's romances were more than sigh-worthy.

Shey hadn't been looking for love. Especially not with a prince. Prince Eduardo Matthew Tanner Ericson of Amar had come to Erie to claim his bride—Parker. But instead he'd claimed Shey's heart.

Shey was rock-hard on the outside, but that was just a veneer. On the inside she was caring, concerned, and so deserved to have a prince.

Cara sighed again. It was all so wonderful.

Her two best friends had found their other halves, men whom they loved and were willing to commit their lives to.

Once upon a time, Cara had thought she'd find a similar path.

For one brief moment three months ago, she'd thought she had.

Mike King.

He'd popped into her life, bringing with him a whirlwind of emotion and hope…hope that she'd found what she'd been looking for. But he'd popped right out of her life again, leaving behind a longing for what-might-have-been.

She'd had just one night, one special night when she'd believed all her fantasies could come true. On that night, she'd believed in love at first sight and happily ever after.

Then it was morning and Mike was gone. In the light of day, Cara awoke to the reality with a thud.

Mike had been just a hazy dream, a misty longing she had thought could grow into something solid. But, like a mist, the morning sun had burned her dream of him away.

But he'd left her something tangible. Something solid and oh-so-real.

The plane touched down and Cara allowed herself one last wistful sigh.

She was going to see to it that Parker and Shey had the most perfect fairy-tale wedding ever.

They'd each have someone to love forever.

And in the end, so would Cara.

Not Mike King. He was just a dream that had come and gone. No, she was going to have a real someone.

She was going to have Mike's baby.

Coming this July from NEXT™

When her teenaged daughter and her eighty-year-old mother both started sneaking out at night, what was a forty-something woman to do?

SANDWICHED by Jennifer Archer

From Jennifer Archer, a humorous tale of the woman in between.

If you enjoyed what you just read,
then we've got an offer you can't resist!

Take 2 bestselling
love stories FREE!
Plus get a FREE surprise gift!

Coming this July from NEXT™

When things don't work out the first time—
there's always Plan B....

THERE'S ALWAYS PLAN B by Susan Mallery

A warm, witty novel from *USA TODAY* bestselling author Susan Mallery and Harlequin NEXT

www.TheNextNovel.com

Four new titles available each month wherever Harlequin books are sold.

HNTAPB

SILHOUETTE *Romance* ®

COMING NEXT MONTH

#1778 THE TEXAN'S RELUCTANT BRIDE—
Judy Christenberry
Lone Star Brides

Thomasina Tyler had no interest in settling down. But the marriage-minded Peter Scholfield had other ideas. For this cautious beauty had captured his interest, and the mouthwateringly handsome executive always got what he wanted!

#1779 FAMILIAR ADVERSARIES—Patricia Thayer
Love at the Goodtime Café

She was the rich girl, he was the rancher's son. And now that she was back in town, the chemistry between Mariah Easton and high school sweetheart Shane Hunter was stronger than ever. But a long-standing family feud would force Mariah to choose between her family and the man of her dreams....

#1780 FLIRTING WITH FIREWORKS—Teresa Carpenter
Blossom County Fair

Mayor Jason Strong was devoted to keeping order in his small town. Only an exotic stranger with an impish glint in her eye was disturbing the serenity of his quiet community. If the handsome widower and single father didn't watch out, the sparks flying between him and the lovely Cherry Cooper might make his peaceful life explode!

#1781 THE MARINE'S KISS—Shirley Jump

Nate Dole had plenty of experience on the battlefield, but that didn't prepare him for Jenny Wright's third-grade classroom! The feisty children had the once-hardened marine thinking twice about the merits of civilian life...especially if it included stolen moments with their alluring teacher.